THE CROOKED INN

Max Mitchell and Dan Evans, two London playwrights, are seeking atmosphere and characters for a play. But when they travel to Wales for inspiration they find more than they bargained for. They arrive in Llanberis on a stormy night, and are forced to stay at the wrong hotel, The Crooked Inn. Then, as they face some disparate characters, and The Crooked Inn's connections to the gaol-break of a murderer, they become involved in a real-life drama of murder and mystery.

ERNEST DUDLEY

THE CROOKED INN

Complete and Unabridged

LINFORD
Leicester

First published in Great Britain

First Linford Edition
published 2008

British Library CIP Data

Dudley, Ernest
 The Crooked Inn.—Large print ed.—
Linford mystery library
 1. Dramatists—Fiction
 2. Hotels—Wales—Llanberis—Fiction
 3. Llanberis (Wales)—Fiction
 4. Detective and mystery stories
 5. Large type books
 I. Title
 823.9'14 [F]

 ISBN 978–1–84782–186–7

Published by
F. A. Thorpe (Publishing)
Anstey, Leicestershire

Set by Words & Graphics Ltd.
Anstey, Leicestershire
Printed and bound in Great Britain by
T. J. International Ltd., Padstow, Cornwall

This book is printed on acid-free paper

1

It was after the train had rumbled beneath the ragged-edge walls of Conway Castle. Max Mitchell's mind's eye was still picturing Conway Estuary, fading away into grey mists. The little town, shadowy and curled like a sleeping cat round the harbour, the lights from the yachts winking across the dark waters. Suddenly he realised he had entered a magic land. A land of mystery where anything, no matter how inexplicable, might happen.

Now they were speeding between the foot of the mountains towering above the train and the sea. The Menai Straits stretching smoothly and glassily towards Anglesey. The late September sky angry with rainclouds. Stars appearing and disappearing as the black, swollen clouds moved lethargically inland. The air over sea and land seemed charged with electricity.

Max thought he caught a flash of lightning on the horizon and Dan Evans, in the corner opposite him said: 'Rain, all right.'

'Looks like a storm brewing.' Max's gaze was fixed on the dark low-lying shape in the sea that was Anglesey, and then a string of lights glimmered at him across the sea.

'Beaumaris,' Dan said. Max was amused by the edge of excitement in the other's voice. It was, Max knew, like coming home for Dan. Though he had been born and bred further south, in the shadow of Cader Idris, it was the valleys and mountains of North Wales which had in his early twenties, won his affection.

The string of lights was cut off by trees which loomed up close to the windows, flashing past in a black silhouette against the sky, as the train swung away from the sea and began to bore into a tunnel. The train was slowing down, the pressure of the brakes could be felt. Dan was on his feet, reaching for his hat and coat. 'Next tunnel after this.'

They roared into the second tunnel,

then the platform was sliding up and a porter was shouting: 'Bangor . . . Bangor.' Max, who had unhurriedly slipped on his raincoat, gave a touch to his hat-brim and grabbed his suitcase. Dan had his suitcase and was clutching a typewriter. The porter, whose disembodied voice they had heard, materialised out of the gloom.

'Porter, sir?'

'No, thanks,' Dan told him. 'We can manage.'

The porter vanished, calling out to someone in Welsh. A gust of wind whistled across the platform, shadowy figures sorted themselves out, carriage doors slammed, there were shouts, the flashing of the green lantern. The train jerked into life once more and pulled away from the platform, its tail-light winked back in the darkness and then it was gone. The platform was deserted.

'Up the steps and over the bridge,' Dan had said and he and Max were among the little straggle of travellers whose footsteps echoed hollowly as they ascended the ill-lit steps to the bridge. 'Hope the car's there.'

Max's watch-dial glowed palely up at him. 'Ten-twenty,' he said.

'Right on the dot,' Dan said. 'Not bad after a five hour run.' He sounded as enthusiastic as if he had driven the train himself.

'Five hours ago we were in smoky old London. Imagine.'

'I'm too busy imagining our pub at Llanberis,' Dan grinned at him. 'And supper waiting for us.'

'I didn't notice you were exactly denying yourself in the dining-car.'

'I know, but I'm hungry again.' They were crossing the bridge now towards the barrier. 'You bring the newspapers?' Dan asked. 'I wanted to read more about that Vernon chap.'

Max tapped with his free hand against the newspapers all folded together which protruded from the other's pocket. 'In your pocket, where you put them.'

'Oh . . . Good.'

Max glanced at him quizzically. 'You still don't see him as a character in the play?'

Dan Evans pursed his lips thoughtfully.

'I think he sounds a type we could use.' His voice rose. 'A ruthless murderer on the run, every hand against him, hunted by the police, scared of his own shadow — '

Max caught the amused expressions of the people around them. 'All right, old chap,' patting the other's shoulder. 'No need to get so worked up about him — you'll have people thinking *you're* a ruthless murderer — '

Dan broke off as he too realised he was attracting attention. 'Was I shouting?'

'Just a trifle.'

They found themselves slowing up with the small knot of people pressing past the ticket-collector. 'All the same,' Dan said to Max from the side of his mouth, 'you must admit it's dramatic enough. Where did they say he was last seen?'

They were on the other side of the gate now, at the head of a flight of steps descending steeply to where two or three cars gleamed in the darkness of the station-yard.

'Chester, I think. Heading towards Liverpool, it was believed.'

Dan nodded, then fixed his attention on the cars waiting. 'Now, where's ours?'

They were half-way down the steps. Max observed a figure approach the foot of the steps and glance up at them expectantly. 'How about this old chap?'

The other followed the direction of his gaze. 'If it is he looks too decrepit to drive a tricycle.'

The figure had shambled hesitantly forward. Now he peered up at them short-sightedly from under ancient bristling eyebrows and then hazarded a respectful touch to the cracked peak of his cap. 'Mr. Evans and Mr. Mitchell?'

Dan surveyed him dubiously. 'You Mr. Price?'

The old man nodded. 'Take your cases, sir — ?' He broke off to sneeze so violently they expected him to fall to pieces. 'Excuse me.'

'But you aren't Mr. Price of Llanberis,' Dan said.

'His father, sir, really. My son's laid up with a sprained wrist. Very painful, it is. Can't drive.'

He was sidling crabwise towards a car

which was backed against the kerb. Max and Dan followed him. Their expressions even more doubtful they observed the car into which he was intent on luring them. It appeared to be almost as ancient as he. It was large and stood high off the ground. The old man opened a door. 'I'll put your suitcase alongside me.'

'How about *him* for a character in the play?' Max muttered irresistibly in Dan's ear.

'We're not writing Rip Van Winkle.' Then to the old man, whose shaky claw-like hands were reaching out for the typewriter Dan said: 'I'll hang on to this.'

They let him take their suitcases which he stacked in the seat beside his own, then climbed reluctantly into the car. Gingerly they sat back. The door closed on them and Price, groaning and grunting, took his place behind the wheel. He gave another tremendous sneeze.

'If he does that again,' Dan said, *sotto voce*, 'the car will fall to pieces.'

'I think the engine's dropped out already.'

The figure in front of them crouched over the wheel, wisps of straggly grey hair sticking over his turned-up coat-collar. Clanking noises and a curiously metallic coughing began to shake the car, followed by the unmistakable sound of the engine running. The noises ceased abruptly. Price crouched again, muttering to himself, at the dashboard. More clanking and metallic coughing. The car awoke into life only to die again. Dan looked at Max. Their faces had sunk into deepest gloom and foreboding. The figure in front bent in an attitude of complete concentration. But apart from an odd scratching sound and a spasmodic cough or two the engine gave no response.

Price leaned back and Dan and Max sensed the dismay he was experiencing. He gave yet another tremendous sneeze whereupon the car engine promptly began running, and they were moving. Max and Dan exchanged amused glances, and then they were turning out of the station-yard and heading down a road that led through the town.

'You know where we're going?' Dan leaned forward.

Price half turned his head. 'What, sir?'

'You know where we're going?'

'Oh, yes, sir.'

'Criccieth Arms Inn, Llanberis.'

'My son told me, sir.'

Dan leaned back and looked out of the window at the darkness lit occasionally by a street-lamp. The car creaked and bumped but kept going. He had stayed at Llanberis a couple of years ago. Young Price had possessed the only car for hire locally and Dan, remembering him when booking accommodation for Max and himself at the Criccieth Arms, had asked the innkeeper to arrange for Price to meet them at Bangor Station. Dan began to recall his previous stay at Llanberis and his expression grew relaxed. The odd little lakeside town nestling at the foot of Snowdon, quiet and peaceful. He turned to the other.

'I'm sure it's just the spot for us to get this play off our chests. Background and plenty of ideas for the very characters we need. In the flesh. I tell you, two weeks and we'll have the epic finished, down to the final curtain.'

'That's the main thing. It's been hanging over us too long.'

Dan pushed his hat on to the back of his head and sank his chin on his chest. His cigarette-lighter flared as he lit a cigarette and dragged at it deeply. Max, who mostly smoked a pipe, which he had not bothered to light up for the last few minutes, caught the speculative look in Dan's dark eyes. The thin, long-chinned features were set, the brow corrugated in thought.

'Don't you agree,' Dan asked, 'this idea of a murderer on the run — like this Vernon chap — coming in at the end of act two would be — ?'

He was interrupted by a flash of lightning which illuminated the road ahead for a vivid, brief moment. Above the rattle and squeak of the car could be heard a low, long growl of thunder. Rain-spots began to appear on the windscreen. The old man gave a grunt and switched on the windscreen-wiper.

Dan turned to Max in mock incredulity. 'Every modern convenience,' he said.

'We might get there tonight, after all.'

The lightning flash had shown them they were now proceeding along a road on either side of which trees, their leaves autumnally bronze, rose up and fell away into the blackness. Above the clank and rattle of the car, came the hiss of the tyres on the wet road. Dan peered out of the window in an effort to estimate where they might be, but found it impossible to make any guess, except that they seemed to be miles from anywhere. Presently the car slowed down, he pressed his nose against the window, trying to see what was happening. Through the slanted rain that reflected the headlamps he thought he could discern a cottage or two, a passing glimpse of a lighted window.

The car's speed decreased and Max queried:

'We here?'

'Don't think so. Why are we stopping, Mr. Price?'

The car jerked to a sudden standstill.

'We've stopped,' Max said.

The figure at the wheel relaxed and turned to them with a sigh of triumph. 'Here we are.' Price slid from under the steering-wheel and he was holding their door open for them to get out. They could see the rain slashing against him as he stood there. Rivulets began to run down his cap-peak and drip on to his nose. Beyond him could be made out the faint glow of curtained windows.

'Are we at the pub?' Dan asked dubiously, but Price appeared not to seem to hear or to hear him incorrectly.

'You gentlemen hurry in, I'll follow with your cases.'

Dan shrugged. They'd better dash for the shelter of the front-door porch which he thought he could make out. He got out of the car, Max following him, the rain driving into their faces, a flurry of wind forcing them to grab at their hats. With Dan, hugging the precious type-writer to him and leading the way, they ran for it. Behind them came Price, muttering what sounded like uncompli-mentary remarks about the weather in Welsh. The porch offered very little shelter and Dan banged the door-knocker impatiently.

They stood for a moment, hearing the

wind whistling round the inn, a swinging sign creaking somewhere overhead and old Price wheezing in their ears. No one seemed to be stirring beyond the door.

'All in bed, by the look of it,' Max said.

'Someone will come in a minute,' the old man encouraged them.

'They'd better. It isn't as if they aren't expecting us.' Dan banged again on the knocker. A few moments went by and they could hear someone approaching on the other side of the door.

'I can hear signs of life,' Max said.

Came the sound of bolts being drawn, a lock turning and the door creaked open. A short, dark, wiry-looking man stood there silhouetted against the warm and welcoming light within. He was in shirt-sleeves and waistcoat, and wore a green baize apron. He peered at them suspiciously.

'What do you want?'

'Being guests here,' Dan said sharply, 'we not unnaturally want to come in.'

'Guests? What names?'

'Look here, d'you mind letting us in out of the wet?' Dan said sweetly. 'Then you can nip along and say Mr. Mitchell and Mr. Evans have arrived.'

'That's it Roberts, *bach*,' Price said, 'tell Josh Jones the gentlemen are here, and they're tired and starved for a bite to eat.'

'And the rain's dripping down the back of my neck,' Max added.

At the sound of the old man's voice the other leaned further out from the shelter of the doorway. 'Mr. Price there, is it?'

'My son's laid up, and I've brought the gentlemen over from Bangor.'

The man called Roberts did not draw back to admit them. His face still bore the same suspicious expression. 'Mr. Jones is busy at the moment. But, anyway,' and his restless eyes fixed themselves on Dan, 'I tell you we've no guests due tonight.'

His voice was drowned in a roll of thunder that echoed and re-echoed before it finally died away in the distance. Dan made a step forward. For a moment it seemed the shirt-sleeved figure would oppose him. Then his eyes flickering uneasily he drew back.

14

'Just while you're making sure we're not expected, we'll come in.'

'Very well,' reluctantly.

The door creaked wider and Max and Dan stood in the dimly-lit lounge of the inn. Price put the suitcases down and hovered in the background. Suddenly Dan turned to Roberts who was closing the door.

'What did you say is the proprietor's name?'

The other eyed him for a moment. Then: 'Mr. Jones, of course. Josh Jones.'

Dan was frowning to himself. 'That's what I thought you said. Funny,' and he threw a look at Max, 'that's not the name I remember.' He regarded Roberts again. 'Is he new, or — sort of temporary?'

The man gave a short laugh. It wasn't a particularly pleasant laugh. 'Mr. Jones has had the Crooked Inn over ten years.'

Dan and Max stared at him.

'What d'you mean, Crooked Inn? Isn't this the Criccieth Arms?' At that moment Price gave a loud sneeze and Dan turned on him angrily. 'Mr. Price, where the devil have you brought us?'

The old man blinked at him nervously. 'Where — where you said, sir. The Crooked Inn, Mynydd Llanberis.'

Dan groaned, then his voice rose angrily. *The Criccieth Arms Inn, Llanberis,* you old — '

'All right, Dan, take it easy,' Max said, catching the look of anguish on Price's face and feeling sorry for the old man.

'The same as I wrote when I ordered the car,' Dan said, his voice dropping onto a more conciliatory note.

Price gulped and wheezed and pushing his cap back from his bristling eyebrows, scratching his head. 'I — I — oh, dear, I am sorry. This cold must have made me a bit hard of hearing. I was sure my son said the Crooked Inn, Mynydd Llanberis. And you, too.'

'I suppose they could sound rather alike,' Max said.

Roberts wore a thin smirk of superior triumph on his dark features. 'Now, perhaps you'll agree you've come to the wrong place.'

'You don't have to look so pleased about it,' Dan was about to continue in the same scathing terms when Max interposed.

'Come on, we'd better be getting along.'

Dan looked at him, shrugged, smiled bitterly. 'All right. Get moving, Mr. Price — if you're sure you've got the right address, *now*. The Criccieth Arms — '

The other's mouth was working noiselessly. Finally he blurted out: 'I'm sorry, sir, but — '

'Now, what?' Dan said irritably.

'I — I — that is, I'm afraid I can't take you — '

'What?'

'What d'you mean?' Even Max's tone was exasperated.

'It — it's the car, sir — '

'What about the car?' Dan, Max could see, was almost beside himself with irritation, he was pushing a hand through his dark hair and scowling. Price turned to him, his mouth working again.

'It won't go, sir,' he explained. 'Not any further. No petrol. I'd forgotten to fill up before I came out, and — '

'For Pete's sake,' Dan rolled his eyes upwards.

Roberts was standing, staring at the old man, his face full of pitying contempt. Max caught his look and decided he didn't particularly care for the man's personality. Then he said to Price: 'Surely you can get some more petrol?'

Price wheezed uncomfortably. 'Not this time of night, sir. Everywhere's closed.'

Max turned to Roberts for confirmation of this, but the man made no comment. Dan was saying to Price:

'You really mean to tell us the car's stuck for the night?'

Price nodded miserably. 'I saw the tank had run dry when we stopped, but I was going to leave the car here till the morning. Come back with some petrol then.'

'If this isn't the flaming limit,' Dan exploded.

Max said half to Roberts: 'Looks as if we *shall* be staying here, after all — '

'You can't stay here.'

Dan turned on Roberts furiously. 'I knew you'd welcome the prospect with delight.'

'We — we haven't got a vacant room,'

Roberts mumbled, and Dan and Max knew he was lying.

'Even if you had,' Dan said, 'you'd cheerfully prefer us to walk to Llanberis in this filthy storm.'

'You couldn't walk, sir,' Price said, with a glance at the man in shirt-sleeves. 'Llanberis is four mile. Soaked to the skin, you would be, and you carrying your suitcases — '

It was Max who asked: 'Why can't we get another car?'

Price considered this for a moment or two. 'Dunno how, it being so late.'

'We'll 'phone round until we do get one,' Dan said. To Roberts: 'Where's the 'phone?'

Roberts' jaw was set, his eyes hard. For a moment the others regarded him silently, then Dan advanced towards him. 'Now, listen — ' but Roberts said hurriedly;

'It's out of order.'

Dan paused and gave the man a narrow look. 'It'd have to be,' he said.

'The 'phone often breaks down when we have these storms.'

'Then it'll have to be the nearest call-box,' Max said. He turned to Price questioningly. The old man shook his head.

'I'm afraid there isn't one for a mile.'

Max listened to the rain driven against the windows by squalls of wind. Thunder still grumbled and rolled about the sky. The prospect of walking a mere hundred yards, let alone a mile, in the darkness of such a night wasn't altogether appealing. Dan was obviously of the same mind, for with a gesture of helplessness he muttered:

'What in hell do we do, Max?'

'Toss up and see who goes to the 'phone-box,' Max reached into his pocket. 'Where's that double-headed penny of mine?'

'Gets more amusing every minute,' Dan said. To Roberts: 'Listen, you, surely — ?'

'Roberts is my name,' the other replied pointedly. 'I'm the waiter here, boots and general handyman.'

'Then, surely you can fix us up just for the night? A bathroom, or the billiard-table — '

'I could sleep on a clothes-line,' Max

said. 'I'm tired enough.'

Price glanced at him sympathetically. He said to Roberts: 'Yes, Roberts, man, Mr. Jones will be able to find somewhere for the poor gentlemen to sleep.'

'Mr. Jones is out. He won't be back till late.'

'I thought you said he was busy?' Dan said quickly.

'Besides,' Max glanced at his watch, 'it's not exactly early now. Surely he'll be back soon?'

'I tell you, he's busy,' the other's voice rose a trifle. 'He's not here, he's out.'

'He certainly picked a good night for it,' Dan said. 'In more ways than one.' Another gust of wind and lashing rain rattled the windows. 'Raining stair-rods, and you can't bear to think of us waiting till your boss does come back and perhaps finding us somewhere to sleep?'

'I — it's not that — ' The other broke off and spun round and the others followed the direction of his gaze.

'Roberts, who's there — ?'

'I'm just coming, Miss Anderson — '

The girl appeared in the curtained

entrance to a passage which led from the lounge. Her red hair glowed vividly in the light. Her face was pale with a wide mouth, and the almond-shaped horn-rimmed glasses she wore gave her an intriguing quality. She came forward, slim and narrow-hipped. 'What's the matter?' glancing from Max to Dan and exchanging good-evenings with them. 'Somebody want Uncle?' Then she saw Price. 'Hello Mr. Price.'

'Good evening, Miss Anderson. The gentlemen do want to see your uncle, as a matter of fact.'

She turned questioningly to Roberts, who remained silent. Dan said to her: 'We want to rest our weary heads beneath his roof for the night.'

'It's my fault, Miss Anderson,' Price volunteered. 'I brought them from Bangor. Thought they wanted to come here, while it was the Criccieth Arms, Llanberis — ' He broke off to sneeze once more. The girl turned to his two passengers.

'What rotten luck for you.'

'We feel pretty low about it,' Max said.

'But your misfortune is our good luck.'

She spoke to Roberts. 'We've got two unexpected customers for the night.'

'There's no room available. I've told them.'

She frowned at him. 'We can't be all that full up, surely?'

'I'm sorry, Miss Anderson. Your uncle told me before he went out.'

But the girl was shaking her head. Max thought she made a strikingly effective picture, in her trim dark grey suit and sophisticated glasses, against the comfortably untidy surroundings of this old Welsh inn, whose walls were built all askew. He gave Dan a quizzical look, but he was much too taken up with the girl to notice it. She was speaking again to Roberts.

'I mean, how can we be full up? Only two people staying here. Miss Kimber and Mr. Darrell. And myself. I'm Wynne Anderson,' she turned to introduce herself. 'I'm staying with Uncle for a few days.'

'I'm Dan Evans. This is Max Mitchell. We don't want to barge in, but if there was an inch of space — '

'Of course, we'll find you somewhere.'

The inn shook as the storm buffeted it. 'You can't go out in this.'

'But, there isn't any accommodation.'

'Don't be so defeatist, Roberts.' She smiled at him charmingly. 'Anyone would think you didn't *want* them to stay.'

Max and Dan threw the other sardonically amused looks. Roberts' mouth set in a thin line. 'I assure you we're perfectly harmless,' Dan said. 'Just a couple of stranded playwrights from London.'

Her eyes behind her spectacles widened with interest. 'Do you write plays?'

'We've been known to try,' Max said.

'I go to the theatre a lot in London. I love it. Have you seen — ?' She broke off. 'But you're tired and hungry.' She turned to Roberts determinedly. 'The Crooked Inn has got two more guests. Even if they have to sleep in *your* bed.'

The man gave a shrug of resignation. 'Very well, miss.'

'There you are,' Price nodded happily to Dan, 'I knew you'd be all right. I'll be getting along, then. You'll be warm and comfortable for the night, now. Be here in the morning I will, with some petrol to take you on to Llanberis.'

He lived in Mynydd Llanberis, not far away it appeared — it was his son, he explained, who lived at Llanberis — and Dan settled up with him and arranged for him to call for them at about ten next morning. After Roberts had closed the door on Price the girl said to Dan:

'Roberts may have misunderstood my uncle. I know he's got the rooms, and he can't *want* to be half-empty.'

'Seems a bit of a waste.'

She turned to Max. 'So we'll see what there is.' To Roberts: 'Bring the gentlemen's suitcases.'

'I'll hang on to this,' Dan said, gripping his typewriter.

Wynne Anderson led the way, followed by Dan and Max, with Roberts, gloomily carrying the suitcases. There was a landing above, running off to the right. 'Have you come up here to write, Mr. — er — ?'

'Evans, Dan Evans. Yes, that's the general idea.'

She nodded and glanced back at Max. 'Watch out for your head. The stairs twist most unexpectedly and you find yourself butting the ceiling. Especially if you're tall.' To Dan, conversationally: 'Perhaps you'll be able to use tonight's happenings to put into your plays?'

'Just the sort of stuff we need. Arriving at wrong hotel late at night. Thunderstorm. Then almost having the door shut in our faces, and — and — '

'And the pretty heroine coming to the rescue.'

She smiled at Max.

Dan glanced at Max and grinned, wishing he'd thought of it himself. But then Max always was the one who came out with the right word at the right moment. Quiet sort, but he didn't miss a trick. Did he, Dan wondered, find the girl attractive? He recalled the famous lines of American poetess, Dorothy Parker: 'Men seldom make passes at girls who wear glasses.' Miss Parker had never met Miss Anderson . . . He said over his shoulder to Max:

'The name of this place, too. The Crooked Inn — there's our title for a start — '

A telephone shrilled somewhere.

Roberts put down the suitcases. 'I'll go and answer it.'

'Thought you said it was out of order?' Dan checked him as he moved downstairs and he paused momentarily without looking back. They watched him cross the lounge and disappear through a door marked: Office. Dan turned to Max. 'He did say it was out of order?'

'Breakdown caused by the storm. He said.'

Wynne Anderson was giving him a puzzled stare. The 'phone stopped ringing and they could hear the murmur of Roberts' voice. Dan answered the girl's questioning look.

'We wanted to 'phone for another car, when old Price told us his had broken down.'

'And he said it was out of order?' He nodded. 'Perhaps he'll explain when he comes back,' she said. Her smile was for them both. 'It does seem to have been a chapter of accidents for you, doesn't it?'

Roberts' voice ceased, they heard the ring of the receiver replaced and in a moment the short, dark figure reappeared. The girl called out to him.

'Who was it?'

'Only the exchange, Miss Anderson. To say the line had been restored again.'

'I didn't know it had been out of order.'

He caught her tone. 'I thought you did.'

As Roberts picked up their suitcases again she gave the other two a look as much as to say they had received a satisfactory explanation of the 'phone incident. 'We must find you your room.'

'If the 'phone's working,' Max said, 'couldn't we get a car to take us to Llanberis?'

She regarded him, Roberts opened his mouth to speak and then Dan cut in. 'Not a chance. Too late for anyone to turn out, especially in this weather.'

'I agree,' she said. 'You'd best make up your minds to stay here. Unless,' with a glance aimed directly at Max, 'you simply can't put up with us, even for a night?'

'It's only that we seem to be giving you so much trouble.'

She led the way past the bedroom

doors which were closed. 'Miss Kimber has got number three . . . Mr. Darrell's number four . . . I'm number five — '

Roberts interrupted her suddenly. 'There's number seven.' Dan and Max eyed him with surprise. 'I — I'd forgotten it was vacated yesterday. Still thinking Mr. Watkins had it.'

She eyed him reprovingly through her glasses. Watching her Dan couldn't make out whether it was because of the spectacles, but her eyes were large and long, with heavy dark lashes. He decided the colour of her eyes was a sort of greenish hazel.

'How could you have made such a mistake, Roberts?' she said. 'Saying there wasn't a room.'

'It was a lapse of memory. And your uncle, too, ordering me — '

She checked him quickly. She indicated the rooms on the other side of the passage further along, and nodded at another closed door. 'Room seven . . . Six is further along round the corner by itself.'

Roberts was opening the door of seven with alacrity. He switched on the light. It was smallish, comfortably furnished. The floor dipped towards one corner, the black, oak-beamed ceiling was uneven and the whole room gave the same impression as the rest of the inn of having been built haphazardly, at any quixotic notion of the builders. There was a wash-stand and water-jug and bowl opposite the two beds, which had a reading-lamp between them.

'Couldn't look less occupied, could it?' Max said.

'I do hope you'll be comfortable,' the girl said.

'No pleasanter sight ever met two weary wanderers' eyes. There's even a table for this.' Dan crossed to a small table in a corner and placed the typewriter on it. 'Though I fancy I'll be able to restrain myself from pounding at it tonight.'

Roberts had put down the suitcases and stood by the door, his expression enigmatic. There was something curiously still and watchful in his attitude, as if he was listening for something. Only a flicker of resentment passed over his face when the girl asked the two others if they would have something to eat before they went to bed. Max said they'd had dinner on the train, while Dan said it did seem a long time ago.

'It's gone eleven, miss,' Roberts said meaningly. Ignoring his hint the girl asked him to prepare some sandwiches. He gave a long-suffering sigh, compressed his lips and went out. 'I'm sorry he seems so inhospitable. But I'm sure he doesn't mean to be.'

They both assured her they, too, were sure he didn't mean to be mean.

'You'll find Miss Kimber in the lounge,' she said, 'having her hot milk. And Mr. Darrell. They're the other guests.'

'Sweet girl,' Dan said after she'd closed the door behind her.

Max agreed, then suggested hadn't they better 'phone the Criccieth Arms and let the proprietor know what had happened to them.

'Funny about that 'phone.' Dan unpacked his suitcase. 'I don't believe it was out of order at all.'

'Only point is, why should the chap

lie?' Max was pouring some water from the jug into the wash-bowl.

'You mean if he wanted to get rid of us he'd have been glad for us to 'phone another car? He could have had some motive we can't guess at.'

'Or, of course, it really may have broken down.'

Dan dismissed the possibility. 'Wonder what he's raked up for us to eat?'

'Afraid he'll have used prussic acid in place of pepper and salt?'

'He's a sinister-looking blighter, though, you must admit.'

'Trouble with you is, you will let your imagination run away with you.'

'Seeing I'm supposed to be a profes-sional playwright, you couldn't pay me a better compliment. Talking of which,' he said, 'didn't I tell you we'd come by plenty of ideas up here?'

He followed Max out of the room. Unimpressed by the other's enthusiasm, Max was saying: 'Including arriving at the wrong pub in the pouring rain — that your idea of a good idea?'

'But, of course, my dear chap. Just

think of the plot you could evolve from the situation we've found ourselves in tonight.'

Max smiled at him, still unconvinced, and they went down the crooked stairs. They did not glance back along the shadowy landing, and so missed the glint of spectacles, behind which two eyes had been watching them from round the corner.

2

Miss Kimber turned out to be a prim, spinsterish-looking woman of indeterminate age. She was sipping her milk with a pained expression before a log-fire burning in the lounge. The stone fireplace was next to the door marked Office. The other guest on the settle on the opposite side of the fire was a plump-faced man, greying hair and wearing rough tweeds. He drank his glass of brandy and warm water with slow appreciation. The glass of milk and the other drink was their customary nightcap, it appeared, which Miss Kimber and Mr. Darrell enjoyed before retiring for the night.

Dan Evans and Max Mitchell had introduced themselves before Dan went off to 'phone the Criccieth Arms. He came back after a few minutes to inform Max the innkeeper had been a bit worried about their non-appearance. He had reacted with sympathetic understanding to Dan's explanation of what had befallen them.

Roberts placed a tea-tray beside the large plate of sandwiches already on a low table. The boots-waiter-general handy-man had removed his baize apron and put on an alpaca jacket. He moved quickly, silently, a wiry, dark figure, still with that air of waiting and listening about him.

'The sandwiches were the best I could do.'

Dan had taken one and started munching it. 'They're very good.'

'Which is more than I can say for this milk,' Miss Kimber complained. Roberts eyed the back of her neck coldly. She went on over her shoulder. 'I've asked you, Roberts, time after time not to bring it to the boil, but just warm it.'

'That's all I did, Miss Kimber.'

'It's so boiling hot I can't drink it.'

Roberts rolled his dark eyes in a long-suffering expression and turned to Max. 'Your tea satisfactory, sir?'

'Excellent, thanks.'

Roberts scowled slightly at the back of Miss Kimber's neck again. But Miss

Kimber was unimpressed by the praise she had heard accorded the sandwiches and tea. 'If I've informed you once, Roberts, I've informed you a dozen times, that to boil the milk is to destroy its nutritive values — '

Roberts spoke across her complaining voice to the plump, grey-haired man. 'Will you be requiring another drink, Mr. Darrell?'

The plump-faced man appeared to jerk his head up with a start. 'Eh? What? No, thanks . . . ' Stifling a yawn as he turned to answer Roberts. 'Must be seeing about my shut-eye.' He gulped off the remainder of his brandy and water.

'Same time in the morning, sir?'

The other nodded and Miss Kimber said to him: 'Off fishing all day again?'

'Nothing else worth while getting up early for, Miss Kimber.' His smile took in Dan and Max. Poising a sandwich half-way to his mouth, Dan said:

'You're keen on fishing?'

'All I think of. Talk of nothing else. Ask Miss Kimber here if I'm not the biggest bore she's ever encountered, when I get going.' Miss Kimber made a protesting murmur, but the plump man went on. 'It's true and I admit it.'

'You exaggerate,' Miss Kimber said over the rim of her glass of milk. 'Though conversation,' with a glance at the other two, 'is rather limited.' Darrell gave a grunt signifying his agreement with her sentiments. 'If it isn't Mr. Darrell's stories of how he caught or didn't catch some poor, defenceless little trout,' Miss Kimber was continuing, 'it's Roberts trying to give me night-mares with his silly gossip about the Crooked Mountain.'

'It isn't gossip, Miss Kimber.'

The woman gave a start and halted, taking another sip of milk to swivel round in her arm-chair. 'I thought you'd gone out, Roberts,' she said. She shook her head and turned back to her milk. 'I've never known anyone keep so silent as you do.'

Roberts' voice had taken on a new tone, there was an edge to it, a quality that might have been a ring of sincerity. His eyes were glittering with a strange, fanatical light.

'What's the Crooked Mountain?' It was Dan speaking through another sandwich.

'This place is built slap up against it,' Darrell told him. 'That's why, as you may have noticed,' with a smile, 'it's built all cock-eyed.'

'We had noticed,' Max said.

'The mountain's called the Crooked Mountain,' his informant continued, 'because it's crooked.'

'As good a reason as any,' Dan said.

'Rises up like a corkscrew,' the other said.

Dan snapped his finger and thumb. 'Of course. I remember hearing about it when I was staying at Llanberis.' He looked across at Max.

'Not one of the biggest of the Snowdon range,' Darrell was saying authoritatively. 'Not by any means. But it's certainly very distinctive.'

Dan nodded. 'Some disused copper-mine, isn't there, half-way up?'

The other nodded affirmatively, and then Miss Kimber gave another startled jump as Roberts, who had been standing silent, staring into space, said: 'Where poor Reuben Thomas died a terrible death.'

He seemed to roll the words round his tongue as if savouring a tasty morsel, and Miss Kimber looked up at him sharply. 'Not again, Roberts, I'm just going to bed.'

'I'm sorry,' he said. But obviously found the topic irresistible, his voice taking on a kind of sepulchral resonance. The wind still whining round the inn, driving the rain slashingly against the windows encouraged him. 'But the storm and strangers at the inn turns a man's mind to eerie things.'

'There's nothing eerie about us,' Max said and Miss Kimber inclined her head towards him gratefully. But Roberts was obviously determined not to be denied.

'I wasn't meaning that, sir,' he said.

'Thanks,' Dan said shortly.

Darrell gave a chuckle, but the glitter did not fade from Roberts' eye. 'It's just the storm howling and the knocking at the door,' he proceeded doggedly, 'makes me think of what it must have been like the night they brought Reuben home for the last time — '

'Trouble with some people is they don't bother to take a grip of their thoughts,' Miss Kimber snapped.

The man on the settle stifled another yawn. 'I think you enjoy trying to make our scalps crawl, Roberts.'

'No, sir,' was the reply, the voice still charged with apparent sincerity. 'Really, I don't.'

Dan, staring closely at him, said: 'Sounds rather intriguing to me, I must say.'

'Now don't encourage him, Mr. — er — Evans — ' Miss Kimber broke off to inquire apologetically: 'You are Mr. Evans, aren't you? And your friend's Mr. Mitchell?'

'Clever of you to remember. People don't remember names, usually, first time they're introduced.'

Darrell said: 'Miss Kimber doesn't let much escape her.'

'What d'you mean?' The woman's tone was suddenly alert. Darrell went on urbanely, however.

'Only that — with all due respect to

40

our two new guests' — Darrell smiled ingratiatingly at Max Mitchell and Dan Evans — 'I couldn't have recalled their names, although I heard them say them as well as you did.'

Miss Kimber took another sip of milk and was silent. It occurred to Max she was regretting her slight umbrage at Darrell's apparently innocent remark. He heard Dan saying how he was just as bad himself, he never could remember people's names, then Miss Kimber glanced up and said:

'Possibly it's my schoolteacher training helps me to concentrate. Besides, I like to know who everyone is.'

'Calling a mental roll-call sort of thing,' Dan said.

'That's one way of putting it.'

'Rather neat way, I thought,' Darrell chuckled.

'Schoolteacher, are you, Miss Kimber?' Dan was making a show of interest, Max thought. 'Where do you teach?'

'Liverpool.'

'Your milk all right now, Miss Kimber?' Roberts was still standing there, looking as if he was awaiting only a momentary lull in the conversation to pounce in with more anecdotal harrowings.

'Not quite so liable to burn the roof off my mouth,' Miss Kimber said. 'But do try and just heat it, not boil it, next time.'

'I do,' Roberts replied obstinately. Receiving from the others a negative response to his question: did anyone else require anything? he started to go. He paused to inform Dan what time breakfast was. From half-past eight to half-past nine and Max agreed they be called at eight.

'Thank goodness he's gone,' Miss Kimber said. 'I was afraid he was going to start on one of his grisly tales again.'

'He really does spin a spine-chilling yarn?' Max said.

'Yes,' Darrell said, 'he knows his stuff all right.'

Miss Kimber gave a shiver and Dan said: 'We must get him talking when you're not around, Miss Kimber.'

'Interested in local legends and ghost stories?' The plump man regarded Max, his expression sleepily curious. He was obviously awaiting the opportunity to make his apologies and take himself off to bed.

'My friend and I are inclined to be pickers-up of unconsidered trifles.'

'Oh, really?' contriving to hide a yawn.

'You aren't newspaper reporters?' Miss Kimber's voice seemed to hold that edgy somewhat suspicious note again. Laughing a little, Dan shook his head.

'I was going to say,' Darrell said slowly, 'I can't imagine there being anything to report in this part of the world.'

'I wouldn't know about that,' Dan replied judiciously. 'Out-of-the-way things can happen in out-of-the-way places.'

Miss Kimber blinked sleepily and spoke through a yawn. 'So long as they don't happen in Mynydd Llanberis. Oh, dear, it's getting awfully late. I really must go to bed.'

They watched her ascend the crooked stairs, trying to hide another yawn, then she was gone. Darrell shook himself and kicked a smouldering log into a few desultory sparks. 'What's the time?' glancing at his watch. He answered his own question: 'Gone half-past eleven. And I'm supposed to be here on a rest-cure. Early to bed and early to rise.' Then, with a look at both of them: 'In these parts on pleasure? Or business?'

'Business, which also happens to be our pleasure.'

'Nice work,' the other nodded. 'If you can get it.'

'We do a bit of typewriter tapping.'

'But I thought you said you weren't journalists?'

'We still aren't,' Max said.

'Playwrights,' Dan explained.

Darrell's eyes widened with interest. 'Write plays, eh?' His gaze flickered from one to the other. 'You mean, you work together?'

'*I* do all the work,' Dan said. 'But,' with a nod at Max, 'he takes half the credit.'

'Not to mention half the money,' Max chimed in agreeably.

'I see . . . ' The plump man chuckled. Now he had risen from the settle, they could see he was of medium height, stocky in his rough tweeds, the shoulders thick and broad. A trout-fly was stuck in the lapel of his jacket. It glistened and caught the light as he moved. 'Afraid I'm not much of a theatregoer. Don't seem to have the time. When I do I like to get out of doors.'

'That must be one of the snags of big business,' Dan said. He took the lid off the tea-pot, saw it was empty, and gave a shrug.

'Don't know about *big* business. But I'm kept pretty busy.'

'Suppose there's always a demand for soap,' Max said. 'Except by small boys.'

Darrell shot him a look and Dan's expression was slightly puzzled. Without concealing his surprise the man in the tweed suit said slowly: 'How do you know I make soap?'

Max raised an eyebrow, as if the question was superfluous. 'Magazine you've been sitting on. *Soap Manufacturers' Gazette.*'

'Pretty sharp of you.' Darrell picked up the magazine and smoothing it out, folded it into his capacious jacket-pocket.

'My friend doesn't miss much,' Dan smiled. 'Still-waters-run-deep type.'

The other gave a little nod. 'So you two have come up here for peace and quiet to write a play?'

'It's the background atmosphere we're after mostly,' Dan said. He warmed to his theme, though Max was convinced the other had asked the question purely by way of making conversation. 'We can always work quietly enough in London. But this is a thriller we're working on, set in a little pub, round about Snowdon.'

Darrell successfully stifled a yawn to exclaim: 'Thriller. Now that's something I do enjoy reading when I get time. Train journeys and that. And there was a thriller play I once saw. Great stuff. Forget what it was called, or who it was by. The actor in it was — ' He sought for the name in his memory, but it eluded him and he gave up. 'Made into a film, it was.'

'In which case it *wasn't* one of ours,' Max said.

'But we'll do a film deal with this one,' he said enthusiastically. 'Sure as my name's not Sam Goldwyn.'

Darrell was looking somewhat out of his depth. 'I hope so,' he said. 'Pity you won't be staying on here. I — I'd like to have sort of watched you at work. Sounds most interesting.' He started for the stairs. 'Must make tracks for bed — ' He broke off to exclaim: 'By God, I do feel all in.'

He gave a sudden stagger, and Dan put out a hand to steady him. The plump face seemed to turn a greyish pallor, and look pinched round the nostrils.

'You all right?' Max asked quietly.

The other's eyes were closed. He was breathing harshly. He bit his lips over a low groan and then with an effort, seemed to pull himself together. 'I — I'm all right,' he said, and forced a smile to his lips.

'You sure?' Dan said anxiously. The other shook Dan's hand off his arm gently.

'It's nothing. Just a sudden twinge, that's all.' He tapped himself over the heart. 'Not all it should be.' His voice was raspy, but he held himself upright and began moving again towards the stairs. 'Why I'm taking things quietly for a bit,' he said. 'Fit as a flea really. Just been overdoing it, the doctor says.'

Dan said lightly: 'These late nights you've been having, that's what.'

Darrell's features seemed less grey. He carried himself with less of an effort as he turned from them, then climbed the stairs, slowly but firmly.

They looked at each other in silence after he had gone. Only the rain still swishing against the windows and squally gusts monotonously moaning round the inn. 'Nice chap,' Dan muttered. 'Must be tough for him to have to take things easy.'

Max was about to say something when they heard Wynne Anderson's voice upstairs. She was bidding Darrell good night.

'Here comes the nice niece,' Dan said.

'No sign of Uncle yet.'

'I do hope you've had all you needed,' the girl said as she came down the stairs. 'Did Roberts look after you properly?' Her smile was warm, her eyes, behind the intriguingly slanted horn-rims, friendly.

'Did us proud,' Dan held out his cigarette-case he had just taken out of his pocket to her. She took a cigarette and he lit it, then his own. 'We were just saying,' he said as he took a deep drag at his cigarette, 'we haven't seen your uncle.'

A shadow flickered across her face. 'No.' She hesitated. 'I was expecting him back before now. I don't know — '

A sudden knock at the front door interrupted her. It startled her so that she dropped her cigarette on to the edge of the table. Dan caught it before it rolled off and she took it from him absently. Max said:

'Perhaps that'll be him.'

She answered without taking her eyes off the door. 'It's not locked. And if it was, Uncle has the key — '

There was a voice outside. 'Open . . . in the name of the law.'

The girl's attitude relaxed and a faint smile appeared at the corners of her mouth as she moved quickly to the door. 'It's Parry the Police.'

The newcomer stood framed in the doorway, the rain behind him shining in the light from the room and glistening on his waterproof cape. 'May I come in?' he said cheerfully and he took off his cape to shake it. Wynne Anderson shut the door behind him.

'It's our local bobby,' she called across to Max and Dan. 'Mr. Parry.'

He was taking off his helmet as he advanced into the lounge. He was a narrow-figured man above medium height, with hair carefully parted over pinkish features and an untidy moustache. He was fortyish and slightly pompous. 'Just passing, Miss Anderson, and saw the lights on.' He nodded to Dan and Max. 'Evening, sirs.' They acknowledged his greeting and he went on. 'Though it's a dirty night to be saying anything good about it, that's a fact.' He smoothed his moustache and said to the girl: 'If I'm intruding I'll continue on my beat.'

'Of course not, Mr. Parry.'

He beamed at her.

'Don't mind us,' Dan said, 'we're off to bed.'

'Didn't think there'd be anyone up, except that Roberts, or perhaps Mr. Jones,' Parry the Police said.

'Uncle isn't back yet. I'm waiting up for him. Roberts has gone up to bed, I think.' She saw his eye was wandering over the tea-things. 'Would you like a cup of tea?'

'No thank you, Miss Anderson,' he said, his tone a trifle abstracted.

'I know you don't drink anything stronger.'

He looked at her, his expression somewhat smug. 'Not when I'm on duty,' he said, 'that's a fact. You never know what may turn up, and I like to be on my toes, and a drop of liquor may make just that difference.' Dan proffered him his cigarette-case, but the other declined it. 'Smoke a pipe, sir. Off duty. Thanks all the same.'

'Get much excitement round here? A poacher or two, I imagine?'

There was an unconsciously condescending tone in Dan Evans' voice which P.C. Parry elected to overlook. 'Poachers, sir? District's full of 'em. There isn't a rabbit in these parts can call its soul its own.' He smirked at the ripple of amusement from the others. 'And cycling without lights,' he went on. 'And — and apple-stealing, of course. Then,' he threw in with elaborate casualness, 'there's this hue-and-cry for Vernon.'

Dan, who'd been about to give Max a discreet wink, as much as to say here's some typically bucolic policeman comedy for you, brought his head round with a jerk.

'I read about him in today's paper,' Wynne Anderson glanced at Max. 'Did you? He'd been seen near Chester, it said.'

'We saw it in an evening paper, coming up in the train,' he said. She gave a little shudder.

'He sounds a horrible brute.'

'Not the sort you'd care to meet on a dark night,' he agreed.

'You any reason to think he's likely to head this way?' Dan asked Parry. The policeman regarded him for a moment, smoothing his moustache slowly. Then he shook his head.

'They say he's making for Liverpool.' There might have been a faint hint of disappointment in his tone. 'After a ship to get away in. No,' he shook his head again, 'this is off his route.'

'Pity.' Dan's comment was drowned by the girl's fervent:

'Thank goodness.'

'I was beginning to wonder,' Max contemplated Parry the Police with an eyebrow raised quizzically, 'if the real reason for your — er — looking in tonight was due to us.'

'You?' It was the girl's puzzled query.

Dan was frowning at Max, who went on, his expression still bland. 'News travels fast in these places.'

'It gets around, sir,' Parry's voice was carefully casual again, but a sudden tension hung in the air.

'I daresay,' Max continued, 'Price may have tipped you off — accidentally, I'm sure — of our arrival. Or,' very slowly, 'someone from here — not so accidentally.'

Wynne Anderson gave a shocked gasp. 'You mean someone here thought — ?'

'For Pete's sake,' Dan yelped. 'Of all the — ' His voice cracked with excitement. 'Roberts, of course — ' He started to laugh, but Parry's level tones interrupted him.

'I did happen to run into Price on my way here. Talking of poachers, that's one of the slyest we've got.'

'Old Price?' Dan asked, with amused surprise.

'Get's his living by it. Good living too.'

'And such a dear old man,' the girl said.

Parry gave a snort. 'Don't know about 'dear.' He's certainly expensive. Top prices he gets for his rabbits — or other people's rabbits — '

Dan swung the other back to the subject under discussion: 'But Price knew quite well who we were,' he said. 'His son must have told him.'

Max put in very quietly: 'Mr. Parry didn't say it *was* Price who tipped him off about us.' To the policeman: 'Did you?'

The other gave him a little grin. 'You're very sharp, sir.'

'Second time someone's remarked that tonight,' Max said.

'You mean that blighter, Roberts?' Dan spoke with a certain vehemence.

The girl glanced at him, then at Max. 'You don't really believe Roberts thought one of you was this horrible man?'

He regarded her carefully. Her expression was somehow guarded by her glasses. It made it more difficult to guess at what she was thinking. Her eyes gave very little away. He wondered if she was genuinely short-sighted, or if she wore spectacles because she was aware of their provokingly mysterious effect. He heard himself tell her: 'The police could best answer that.'

At his non-committal reply she swung away from him impatiently, thrusting her hands into her pockets. Dan gave her a mocking grin and then with a nod at Parry asked Max:

'Wonder which of us he thinks looks most like Vernon?'

'You,' Max replied promptly. 'Typical killer's ears.'

The tension was broken. Parry guffawed. It was an infectious laugh, and even Wynne Anderson found herself smiling as she said: 'Mr. Parry, was it Roberts?'

He answered her with a certain gravity. 'I don't think it's very important who it was, miss. They felt it was their duty, and — well — they *might* have been on to something.' He caught Max's eyes and chuckled again.

'I take it,' Dan asked him, 'you're not going to snap the bracelets on us — yet?'

The other shook his head solemnly. 'Neither of you two gentlemen answers the description, that's a fact.'

Dan's face sagged slightly so that the girl said: 'You look disappointed.'

'Thinking it might be publicity for our play, I shouldn't wonder,' Max said.

'Max,' Dan said, 'how could you — ?'

Parry was looking from one to the other, puzzled. Wynne Anderson said: 'Mr. Mitchell and Mr. Evans are writing a play.'

The other's face lightened with understanding. 'Very absorbing occupation, I'm sure,' he said sententiously, 'we had an artist staying in the village, two summers ago.' Then, 'Your uncle not about, did you say, Miss Anderson?'

'He isn't in, as it happens. Though he should be back any minute. Did — did you want to see him?'

'No. Just wondered how he was keeping.'

'I'll tell him you were here, Mr. Parry.'

Dan said: 'I'm sure we shall all sleep easily in our beds, now we know you're protecting us.'

Parry the Police eyed him for a moment. 'Thank you, sir, I hope you'll both have pleasant dreams.'

'I'll come out with you,' the girl said, 'and see if Uncle's coming. The storm seems to have dropped a bit.'

The door opened, and the night sounded calmer. The glistening lines of rain no longer slanted against the darkness beyond, the whistle of the wind had died to an occasional whimper. As Parry and the girl stood outside talking, Dan muttered to Max:

'Nothing of the village cop about him.'

'He seems to know how many beans make five.'

'Wonder who it was 'phoned him?' Dan kept his voice low.

'Roberts is the likeliest, certainly.'

'On another 'phone. Probably is one, somewhere.' Max gave a murmur of agreement and the other went on. 'Why he didn't want us to try for a car. Suddenly thought one of us might be that chap, and he meant to keep us here, even if we did stay the night — '

'Doesn't explain why he tried to slam the door in our faces first.'

'Didn't *like* our faces.' They heard the girl's goodnights to the policeman and Dan glanced in her direction. 'By the way, hope her uncle's all right. She seems a bit worried about him. Oddish, don't you agree, his being out this sort of night?'

'Perhaps he does a spot of poaching on the side — '

Max broke off as the front door closed and the girl came towards them. 'Poor Mr. Mitchell and Mr. Evans, first one thing and then another.'

'Everything happens to us,' Dan said to her nonchalantly. 'It has its amusing side.'

'You were both very good-tempered about it.'

'Any sign of your uncle?'

'Not yet.' She said something about the storm having subsided, there were comments upon Parry the Police.

Conversation seemed to come to a cul-de-sac and they were saying good-night and she was left to await the return of her uncle while the two others went to their room.

'Wonder which is her uncle's room?' Dan asked sleepily, pulling off his shoes, and getting no reply, went on: 'And Roberts'?' But Max was too engrossed with the prospect of bed to bother with his mutterings. Dan looked across fixedly at the other and said: 'I'm glad we stayed.'

'Better than walking to Llanberis, I admit. Though I still think we should have tried to 'phone for a car.'

Dan wasn't listening. 'Damn glad we stayed.'

Max eyed him curiously. 'You thinking about the girl?'

'Me? It's you made a hit with her.'

'Rubbish. You're just her type.'

'I tell you, it's the long, craggy sort she's mad for. But it wasn't her I'm thinking about. No, it was when Roberts came back and said the 'phone was working again.'

'Was it?' Sleepily, without the faintest

idea what the other was talking about.

'That was when I got the brainwave.' Max was looking for a slipper he seemed unaccountably to have left behind. 'Max,' Dan's voice was serious, 'haven't you got the atmosphere here?'

'I've got my slipper,' and Max retrieved it from under the bed, where he had unwittingly kicked it. The other threw him a dirty look and went on tenaciously.

'This twisted old inn built all askew against a corkscrew mountain. And the people in it. Spinster schoolteacher on holiday — ' He broke off. 'Holiday, she says, and school holidays are over.' Max blinked at him as Dan continued. 'Poor devil of a soap manufacturer, probably dying on his feet — '

'I'll die on *my* feet if I don't get to sleep,' Max warned him, but without avail.

'Not to mention the porter-cum-head-cook-and-bottle-washer. Suave, sinister, sly-faced liar. Then old Price, who turns out to be the local champion poacher. And this murderer — what's-his-name — and Parry, the village cop. Somebody 'phoning him about us.' Max had got into bed. 'Then, the girl,' Dan went on. 'Attractive, red-haired and those intriguing glasses she wears. But worried, behind all her alluring mystery — '

'Oh, shut up — '

'Yes, worried,' wagging a finger at him. 'It's her uncle, out late on a storm-swept night.' He moved round and sat heavily on Max's bed. 'Don't you get it my dear chap?' He stood up, waving his arms excitedly, and began pacing between the beds.

'I wish you'd get into bed and stop stamping up and down like some ham actor.'

The other turned on him. 'Here's a smash play rammed right down our throats, and — all you can do,' as Max yawned unrestrainedly, 'is yawn at it.'

Max stopped yawning. 'Play? Putting a real place and real people into the plot. The idea of a murderer on the run — this chap, Vernon — yes,' he conceded, 'perhaps we could work him in — '

The other ignored him. 'We'll use this very pub, and everyone in it. We'll even use the name. I said the Crooked Inn was a terrific title, and it damn well is.'

Max rubbed his lean chin. 'Come to think,' he muttered slowly, 'it isn't a bad title.' Dan sat heavily on his bed again. 'Business man,' Max said thoughtfully, 'whose doctor's warned him he must take things easily — '

'And the schoolteacher,' Dan broke in. 'And Roberts. A perfect crook type.'

Max eyed him and spoke slowly. 'It could be, you know.'

'I tell you, it's a hundred per cent.'

'The idea would be,' Max's gaze narrowed, 'to build up each character so the audience think he or she is the precise opposite of what they turn out to be. And we could work a double twist. Example, Darrell doesn't realise he's fatally ill, though everyone else knows it — '

'Then at the curtain, there *isn't* anything wrong with him.'

'I have a feeling coming over me,' Max said, caught up by some of the other's excitement. 'A warm, standing-room-only feeling — '

'Have to keep the girl on the level,' Dan

said judiciously. 'Love-interest.'

'She could be a crook against her will,' Max suggested.

'Didn't I tell you we were coming to the right part of the world?' Dan Evans said. 'Where else in the world could what's happened tonight happen? Nowhere else but in these amazing mountains. Where else would you find old Price, Parry the Police — ?' He stood up and tying his dressing-gown sash said: 'I'm going to find the bathroom.'

'Just a little way along the landing,' Max told him. 'Noticed the sign when we came up.'

From the door Dan said: 'Get a pencil and a piece of paper and start making notes. We'll start work on it tonight.'

'One idea you'll find me working on,' Max said, 'is sleep.'

'Sleep,' scornfully. 'We're going to *work*.'

Max shook his head to himself as the door closed on the other. He yawned, and slid down into the bed. He felt he would need matchsticks to prop his eyes open any more. Involuntarily he began asking himself if this new idea for the play was something. The setting of a strange, sinister inn had been used before. But with this twist to the characters? That was new, original, he felt confident. He was beginning to wonder drowsily, if they really had got the makings of a hit on their hands, when the door opened suddenly and Dan stood there.

'What in hell's the matter?' Max was jolted into wakefulness by the other's expression. 'You look as if you've seen a — '

Dan closed the door and spoke unnaturally quietly. 'That room, the one round the corner. I — I just took a look-see inside. Don't know what made me. Some impulse — '

'Shouldn't be so damned nosey.'

But Dan wasn't smiling. 'Thinking about this new plot, or something — ' He broke off and drew a deep breath.

'Give you any new ideas?'

'It did.'

Max still kept his tone light. 'What did you see in there? A body?'

'There was a body, all right.'

Max sat upright in the bed. 'I'll buy it,' he said. 'Whose? No, don't tell me, let me guess — ' He corrugated his brow extravagantly. 'I know, the uncle's.'

The light fingers of the quietening wind shook the windows, a last defiant gust of rain spattered the panes. The swinging sign creaked gently, somewhere a floorboard squeaked, an old beam gave a low growl as the inn prepared to settle down for the night.

'Vernon, the murderer,' Dan said. 'He's sitting there in a chair. Asleep.'

3

'You know,' Max Mitchell said slowly, 'this imagination of yours will be the death of you.'

He swung himself out of bed and pushed his toes into his slippers. The other was facing him, the colour returning to his features, though he was still slightly glassy-eyed, as if what he had seen still remained before his vision.

'I tell you, he's in number six.'

'Vernon?'

Dan nodded. 'Sitting in a chair, fast asleep.' He took a deep breath. 'If you still think it's my imagination working overtime, come and take a peek for yourself.'

Max continued to stare at him disbelievingly. After all, they'd only seen Vernon's photo in the papers. It was a definite type of face, but even so this chap Dan had encountered could have been someone like him. He suggested as much, but the other shook his head decisively.

'No one else could have owned that face.'

Max was pulling on his dressing-gown, his brows drawn together. Dan appeared convinced he'd seen what he'd seen. Hallucination or whatever, all Max felt he could do was humour him. 'He didn't wake up?' he asked.

'Probably wouldn't be here if he had. I'd opened the door quietly, the light was on and I got a real look at him. Then I hopped it while the going was good.'

'Suppose I had better take a look myself.'

Dan caught the lack of conviction in the other's manner. 'I know you still think I dreamt it,' he said good-humouredly. 'Come on then.'

There was no one about. The light in the lounge below was dimmed. The landing itself was lit only by a small bulb over the notice which indicated the direction of the bathroom. The floorboards creaked though they made their way as quietly as possible along the shadowy passage. But they seemed to disturb no one. Room six was round the corner. It occurred to Max anyone might easily have thought it was the bathroom, the notice was a trifle confusing. The door was closed.

'I'll open the door,' Dan whispered. There was a faint squeak as the door swung back. The room was dark. 'Someone must have put the light out,' Dan said. He decided to risk putting the light on again, though it might wake the figure in the chair. There was a click of the light-switch.

'For Pete's sake — '

'Vernon the murderer,' Max murmured dryly.

There was no one there.

'But, I tell you — ' Dan was utterly baffled. 'That's the chair he was sitting in.'

'I'm sure it was, old chap,' Max told him kindly.

As the other started to say something, a movement behind their backs brought them wheeling round. Roberts stood there in the shadows.

'Are you looking for your room?' he inquired silkily. 'Seven is your number.'

'I know,' Max said hurriedly. 'We —
that is — ' While he tried to think of
something to say Dan blurted out:

'Who's got this room?'

'This room, sir? No one is occupying it.
No one at all.'

'But I saw someone here, a few minutes
back.'

'I don't think you could have done,'
the other's reply contrived to sound at the
same time firm and deferential. 'Unless
Mr. Darrell, or Miss Kimber came in here
for some reason — '

'It wasn't either of them.'

'Then there couldn't have been anyone.
They're the only people staying here
— apart from yourselves — Miss
Anderson's downstairs.'

'He was asleep in that chair.' Dan's
voice rose. 'I recognised him at once — '

'Take it easy, Dan,' Max cut in. 'You'll
wake everyone up. As Roberts says,' he
went on, giving the other's arm a
meaning grip, 'you must have been
mistaken.' Dan opened his mouth to
protest he hadn't been mistaken, when
the pressure on his arm tightened. 'Mr.

Evans is over-tired, Roberts. Worked up a little over this play of ours.'

'I understand, sir.' Roberts' face was Sphinx-like. Once more Dan opened his mouth. The grip on his arm became vice-like.

'Mr. Evans was looking for the bathroom,' Max continued, 'and opened this door in error. Thought he saw someone — er — we — er — know. A friend,' he said glibly. Dan made another attempt to speak.

'I was only going to say — '

'Let's get back to our own room.' And Max was urging the other along the passage, calling a good-night over his shoulder to Roberts. 'Just an optical illusion, old chap,' he was rattling on as he and Dan headed back the way they'd come. 'Happens to all of us, nothing to worry about. Especially when you're overworked. Good night's rest and you'll be all right in the morning.' He glanced over his shoulder as he opened the door of their room. The shadow of Roberts was thrown on the wall.

'I was only going to say,' Dan managed

to speak as the door closed behind them, 'I was sorry I dragged you out for nothing.' He was ruefully massaging his arm where the other had gripped him.

Max gave him a look which was somewhat veiled, then pulled off his dressing-gown and with a: 'Forget it,' jumped back into bed.

Dan was shaking his head thoughtfully at his pillows as he scuffed off his slippers. 'Extraordinary, you know. I could have sworn — '

'Forgive me butting in when you started to tell Roberts,' Max said.

'Damn glad you did.' Dan climbed wearily between the sheets. 'I was going to blurt out how I'd seen Vernon and everything. He'd have thought I was either tight or nuts.' His voice was subdued as he went on puzzling it out. 'And it wasn't as if I was thinking of Vernon at the time.' There was no reply and Dan raised his head to glance across at the other bed. 'Afraid I've been a bit of a bore. Sorry and all that.'

There was still silence and then Max said between yawns: 'Just one of those things — ' his voice trailed off sleepily. 'Could have happened equally as well to me.'

'Anyway, it's an idea we could use in the play, perhaps.'

'Might.' But Max sounded preoccupied. 'I was getting round to another twist in the plot, when you bounded in.'

'We must talk about it in the morning,' Dan said drowsily. 'Wonder what Roberts made of it?' he yawned, he was barely awake now. 'Probably put me down as one of those wild, temperamental authors.' His voice trailed away. 'I can imagine the sort of yarn he'll spin the nice niece . . . '

Roberts had, in fact, found those almond-shaped hornrims watching him from the lounge as he came downstairs after Max Mitchell and Dan Evans had returned to their own room. She had heard someone moving about.

'It was the two gentlemen. One of them thought he saw someone in number six — '

'What was he doing there? They're in seven.'

'Mistook it for the bathroom. So I understand.'

She glanced at the dark, secretive face, but there was nothing there to suggest he was keeping anything back from her. 'Which one was it thought he saw whoever it was in six?'

'Mr. Evans.'

'And he and Mr. Mitchell have gone back to their own room now?'

'Yes, Miss Anderson. Mr. Mitchell explained to me his friend was a bit over-tired and was suffering from an hallucination.'

She bit at her lower lip in puzzlement. Suddenly a thought occurred to her. Just as she was about to put it into words, there was the sound of someone humming a hymn-tune and footsteps outside. The front door was flung open.

'Uncle, at last.' She hurried to him, and searched his bearded face anxiously. 'Are you all right?'

'You not in bed?' he said, pretending to scowl at her. She nodded towards Roberts who was locking and bolting the door after him.

'We've been waiting up for you.'

His straight, rather grimly chiselled mouth softened. 'Your pretty head should be full of dreams, my dear. Not worrying about me.' He slipped out of his raincoat, which was only slightly damp and handed it and his thick cap to Roberts, who disappeared with them.

'It's been such a storm,' she said. 'You didn't get drenched?'

She followed him over to the fire. He pushed a rubber boot against a log, and caused some sparks to splutter for a few moments, then the flame died away. 'Not a bit,' he reassured her, smoothing his thick, black hair, greying at the temples, with strong fingers. 'That's what made me so late. Had to shelter at a friend's house.' His voice was rich, the Welsh lilt of it melodious and resonant. He gave a little laugh and pressed a hand on her shoulder. 'You see, I'm safe and sound, Wynne, so you can sleep in peace.'

He glanced up as Roberts returned and stood as if waiting. A shadow flickered across Josh Jones' face and then it was gone and he was smiling at the girl again.

74

'Oughtn't you to have something — a hot drink — before you go to bed?'

'Now, Wynne, my child, don't you bother over me any more. Off to bed with you. I'm all right, never fear.'

'I'm glad you're back anyway. By the way, we've got some news for you,' with a glance at Roberts, 'haven't we?' She didn't notice Roberts shift uneasily from one foot to the other as she continued. 'Two more guests.'

Josh stiffened a little, his beard jerked forward at her. Then he wheeled round on the man beside him. 'What's this?'

'*He* didn't want them to stay,' Wynne said quickly. 'Something about you'd said there wasn't any room.'

He eyed her cautiously. 'I see,' he said to her slowly. 'Well . . . quite, my dear.' His manner became genial again.

'Two men from London,' she said. 'Old Mr. Price got muddled and brought them here by mistake. Then the car broke down — '

'That's why his car's outside? I wondered what it was doing there.'

'It's been a night of excitement, Uncle.

Hasn't it, Roberts?'

'It has, miss.'

'What with the storm, those two arriving, and the 'phone out of order, then Mr. Parry calling.' She gave a little laugh, and her spectacles flashed. 'To make sure Mr. Mitchell or Mr. Evans — those are your new guests — wasn't the murderer — what's his name — ?'

'Vernon?'

The name came from the bearded man as an involuntary gasp, he seemed to have been caught off his guard. The amusement vanished from her face. His hand pressed her shoulder again.

'It's nothing,' he replied. 'Nothing. Only what I've read about him in the paper.'

'You didn't think he might be in this part of the world?'

His hand was suddenly heavy. Staring up into his sombre face she sensed Roberts standing perfectly motionless. The inn had become deathly silent. Then her uncle's touch was lighter, his eyes kindled. 'Why should he make for Mynydd Llanberis?' he asked easily with a glance at Roberts. 'So Parry the Police was here, was he?'

'Seems Mr. Price, or someone told him about those two.' Roberts jerked his head in the direction of the bedrooms. Wynne, who had been looking at him, turned back to Josh.

'He wouldn't know what to do with a murderer,' the latter scoffed, 'if he met one.'

'Let's hope he doesn't meet one, for his sake and perhaps ours.'

He gave her a faint smile. 'Don't you worry, he won't. Not this Vernon chap, if that's what you're thinking of. Most likely trying for Liverpool, they say. Eh, Roberts?' Josh Jones was gently urging the girl towards the stairs. 'So off to bed you get, my dear, and your mind easy.' She slipped her arm into his. At the foot of the staircase he added: 'Thanks for taking care of the inn while I was away.'

'I did what I thought best.' She saw Roberts had taken a stub of cigarette from behind his ear and was lighting it. 'I couldn't think you'd want to turn people away, when you had the rooms empty.'

'Afraid Roberts must have misunderstood me.' She caught his wink as if he was telling her confidentially: you know what these servants are, and she smiled back at him. 'Nos *da*, Wynne *bach*,' he said.

She replied, in the little Welsh she had learned: 'Nos *da*. Good night, Roberts.'

She was gone and Josh Jones started humming the hymn-tune to himself. Roberts crossed slowly to the stairs. He stood listening. Then apparently not satisfied, he moved up quickly and silently and stared in the direction of the bedrooms. The other watched him, still humming to himself. After a few moments Roberts came downstairs taking a deep drag at his cigarette-stub. Slowly expelling a spiral of smoke he said softly:

'I tried to drive them away, but she wouldn't let me.'

The other made no reply for a moment. He shook his head slightly from side to side, in answer to his own thoughts. They did not seem to be very pleasant thoughts, by his corrugated brow. 'They *would* have to turn up tonight,' he said, as if speaking aloud to himself.

The other shrugged. 'Nothing I could do about it' he threw a glance upstairs again. 'Not without arousing suspicion.'

'Who are they?' Josh kept his voice low.

'Playwriters or something. Staying the night, they are.'

'Think that's who they are really? They couldn't be — ?' The query faded away. As Roberts gave a non-committal shrug the bearded man took a step forward. 'What d'you mean?'

'Just before you came in, one of 'em was in number six — '

Josh gave a low hissing gasp. 'Did he — ?' he broke off to throw a look upstairs. 'What was that — ?' His voice was harsh with suspicion and fear.

Roberts drew coolly at his cigarette-stub. He appeared to be enjoying the other's distress. There was an expression of contempt on his lips. There remained little suggestion of servant and employer between them now. Josh gained the foot of the stairs.

'Thought I heard someone.' He went

slowly up, paused half-way indecisively. 'Anyone there?' he called in a low voice. 'Anyone there — ?'

No reply, no sound or movement from above. 'It's no one,' Roberts assured him. The other made as if to go on up the stairs, then decided his fears were unfounded and descended slowly.

'Let's go into the office. We can be overheard here.'

Roberts eyed him for a moment, took the cigarette-stub out of his mouth, spat a loose fragment of tobacco at the floor, then tossed the stub into the fire. He followed Josh into the office. He left the door slightly open.

'This fellow, you say,' Josh still kept his voice low, 'looked in at number six. So he must have seen — ' he hesitated as if loath to complete the sentence and a film of perspiration glistened on his brow, '*he must have seen Vernon?*'

'Keep your hair on. As luck would have it, I heard this chap, Evans, come out of seven, which he and his pal are sharing. I decides to keep an eye on him, and he goes and makes for number six — '

'How could he have known? He must be a cop — '

'I'm not sure,' Roberts muttered thoughtfully. 'I don't think so.'

The office was small, and both men leaned against a desk, above which hung a green-shaded electric-bulb. The desk stood against a curtained window, with, on the wall opposite the door, several shelves of miscellaneous files, hotel-trade reference-books, time-tables and other volumes. Behind the two men was a narrow, cloth-covered table beneath a stuffed trout in a glass case. Two or three calendars, bearing advertisements, on the walls. A telephone stood on the desk. In one corner a fishing-rod in its case next to a double-barrelled gun.

'Listen,' Roberts said. 'This chap finds Vernon asleep, the light on — fool had dozed off — no mistake who he is, to anyone who's had a good look at his picture in the papers. He goes back to tell his friend, which gives me the chance to nip in and slip Vernon into my room. Just in time.'

The other gave a grunt of thankfulness

and Roberts continued:

'Then I watches to see what Mr. Nosey Parker will do next. Sure enough he comes out with the other one. He can't believe his eyes when he finds the room empty.'

'What happened?'

Roberts pulled a crumpled packet of cigarettes from his pocket and took a cigarette out. He lit it from a cheap, metal lighter. He drew at it slowly before he went on with his story. 'I decides to butt in, then,' he said, and described the scene between him, Max and Dan in room number six.

'You don't think they were bluffing *you*?'

'That did occur to me, don't you worry.' Roberts shook his head. 'But the more I think about it, the more I believe they weren't. Way they acted, their attitude.'

'I knew it was too risky, letting Vernon come here.'

'Paid to take risks, aren't you?'

Josh gave Roberts a long, level look. 'It isn't what I'm paid.'

'More of a case of being under a certain someone's thumb — I know.'

The other's eyes blazed, angry words rose to his lips, but he choked them back, he leaned on the desk in an attitude of hopelessness. 'All the money in creation wouldn't have tempted me to help this blasted scheme.'

'Our friend's smart enough to pick the right sort.' Roberts tapped the ash off his cigarette, his face unmoved. 'Them who won't blab, because they *can't* not without landing themselves in the soup, too.'

'Having my inn used for those others was bad enough, but a — a murderer. And a swine like this one.'

'Doesn't sound a nice piece of work exactly. But he can pay, so . . . ' Roberts blew a cloud of cigarette smoke ceiling-wards. Then: 'What state was the mineshaft in?'

'Another storm like tonight's and the whole thing'll collapse.' Josh's bearded chin jutted forward and he said through clenched teeth: 'And I hope it does.'

Roberts slanted a look at him. 'Why

don't you fix it to happen when you-know-who is there?' he suggested.

'You think of everything, don't you?'

'You got to — if you want to live.'

'I've done some things in the past, I know,' Josh's eyes staring unseeingly at the curtains. 'I wanted to make quick money. Easy money. But murder, never.' The knuckles of a clenched fist with which he pressed on the desk whitened. 'And the thought of helping this swine upstairs sickens me to the stomach.'

Roberts gave him a speculative look. 'What's got into you, tonight? All on edge and nervy — haven't even asked me if I'd like a drink, neither.' The other pushed himself away from the desk, as if his heavy shoulders could scarcely bear the weight of his bowed head. 'Give yourself one, too,' Roberts said, 'buck you up.'

Josh produced a whisky bottle and two glasses from a cupboard, and placed them on the table. While he turned back for a syphon of soda, Roberts was pouring himself a stiff whisky. He held the glass out to the soda-syphon with a cautionary: 'Don't drown it.'

Josh mixed himself a drink and sloshed it slowly round his glass. 'You hear anything tonight?' he asked. 'About — ?'

'I'd have tipped you off right away, wouldn't I?'

Josh inclined his head affirmatively. 'That must mean there's still some delay,' he said.

Roberts jerked a thumb at the window. 'Likely to be while this weather lasts.'

'It's this having to wait which is so dangerous. If *both* of them upstairs had seen Vernon you wouldn't have been able to bluff it out.'

'Always a question of luck in this game. If there wasn't, if things went exactly to our plan, police would never make a pinch.'

Josh finished his drink and put down the glass. 'You can be cynical,' he said. 'You've only got yourself to worry about.'

'He travels fastest who travels alone,' Roberts' expression was smug. 'That's what they say.'

'Whether the road leads to hell or heaven, eh?'

The other scowled at him. 'Now you're getting morbid.'

Josh Jones pushed his hands deep into the pockets of his double-breasted jacket.

He was about to speak when they heard Wynne Anderson calling quietly. He moved to the door quickly, conscious of Roberts swinging round with a startled exclamation.

'Hope she hasn't been listening,' Roberts said hoarsely.

'Of course not. You wait here.' Josh called out to the girl: 'All right, my dear.' Opening the door wide he went into the lounge. Wynne was at the foot of the stairs. She was wearing a plain dressing-gown.

'I didn't hear you come upstairs and I wondered if you were all right.'

He patted her hands in his. 'Roberts and I are talking.'

'I thought I heard his voice.' She glanced at the office door. 'Forgive me, only I felt worried about you. Silly of me, I know.'

'There's nothing about me for you to lose any sleep over,' he said gently.

'Perhaps it's all the excitement tonight. And Parry mentioning that dreadful man.'

'Vernon?'

She regarded him levelly for a moment. 'You're not trying to hide anything from me, are you?'

'Hide anything?' he asked quickly, too quickly. 'What d'you mean?'

'Why do you seem so worried, why aren't you like your usual self any more?'

'Now don't you bother about me, even if I am a little moody at times. It's nothing more than the usual business irritations.'

She turned back half-way up the stairs and whispered, with a glance at the office: 'And don't sit up too late talking with Roberts.'

He went back slowly to the office, humming the same old hymn-tune as he stood in the doorway of the office, watching unseeingly as Roberts helped himself to another whisky and soda.

'Everything okay?' Roberts asked quietly, without looking up from his drink.

The other pushed the door shut with his foot. He stopped humming to himself and squared his shoulders, so that he seemed to tower over Roberts. He spoke slowly, his tone very low, so that Roberts only just caught the words.

'I'm not going through with it,' Josh Jones said.

'Not going through with what?'

'Vernon. I'm not going to lend a hand to help him escape.'

Roberts' eyes narrowed until they were bright slits. He put down his glass on a corner of the table deliberately. 'You gone out of your senses?'

'I've come *to* my senses.'

The other faced him, his lips drawn back over his teeth in a wolfish snarl. 'You mean, you're going to doublecross us?'

Josh regarded him calmly. 'Put it in those words you like. I prefer to think I'm doing the straight thing.'

'Look here, you blithering old idiot — '

'I'll trouble you to choose your words more carefully,' Josh's voice was like a whiplash, 'or I'll — '

Roberts cringed back. 'All right, all right,' his manner more conciliatory. 'I'm sorry — only you're talking like a fool if you fancy you can put one over — '

'I shall go to the police.'

'So now you're going to the cops. And what, if it isn't a rude answer, are you going to tell them?'

'Where they can find someone they want.'

Roberts slammed down his fist on the desk in ungovernable fury. At that moment the telephone rang and Josh dropped his hands, his face filled with sudden alarm. 'Who can that be?'

'Best way to find out is answer it. Here,' Roberts said, as the other made no move, 'I will . . . Hello? This is the Crooked Inn. Second time you've rung in the last hour to tell me that. Well, it's *still* in order.' He slammed down the receiver, grumbling to himself: 'Suppose they haven't got anything better to do.'

'Who was it?'

'Exchange. To say the 'phone's in order. They 'phoned through earlier to tell me the same thing.'

'Probably breakdowns elsewhere reported,' Josh's expression relaxed, 'and they wanted to check.'

'Anyway,' Roberts bared his teeth in another wolfish grin, 'you don't have to call on Parry the Police in person, you can 'phone him.' He indicated the 'phone.

'I'm not afraid to face the police.' With quiet dignity. 'Not now.' Roberts realised Josh was deadly serious. 'You make me sick,' he exploded. Then he said suddenly: 'And what do you think I'll be doing? Or do you think I've gone crazy like you, too?'

'Do what you like.'

'You don't really believe I'm going to let you get away with it,' Roberts said incredulously, 'without raising a squawk?'

'How can you stop me?'

Roberts drained his drink and drew his sleeve across his mouth. 'Someone else may have an idea or two about that,' he said. 'Who isn't a hundred miles away, remember?'

But the bearded features remained unperturbed. The heavy shoulders were squared as if they had thrown off a heavy load which had long been weighing them down. 'I shouldn't try and warn Vernon,' Josh said. 'I've got the only key to his room, and,' his tone grimly resolute, 'I'm going to turn the lock. Now. There's no other way out — the window jams, won't open wide enough — '

'Why, you blasted — '

Roberts crouched as if he were about to spring, but the other faced him rock-like and master of the situation. 'If you try and prevent me,' Josh said coolly, 'you'll only wake everyone. Then the cat will be out of the bag.'

Roberts relaxed and leaned back against the table, staring at the other with veiled eyes. 'Got it all planned, eh? You're a cool customer,' he admitted grudgingly, 'I give you that.'

'The same applies to anyone else who starts any rough stuff,' Josh Jones continued warningly. Deliberately he turned his back on the other and moved slowly towards the door.

For a moment Roberts looked again as if about to hurl himself in a vicious attack at that broad, self-confident back. Then he thought better of it.

Instead, in a low, persuasive voice: 'D'you realise what you're doing, man? You're going to bust the set-up wide open.'

'I hope so,' came the unruffled reply over the thick shoulders.

'And you know what you'll be doing besides?' Something in the other's tone caused Josh to turn at the door, his heavy beetling brows raised questioningly. 'Signing your own death-warrant,' Roberts whispered hoarsely.

Josh Jones stared at him unwinkingly for a long moment then without a word swung round and went out of the office, humming the hymn-tune to himself.

4

Dan Evans was suddenly wide awake, staring into the darkness and making out the faint glimmer along the top of the badly-fitting door from the light on the landing outside. He lay there and heard a grandfather clock chime twice. Two o'clock. What the devil had dragged him up from the unconsciousness in which he had been blissfully floundering? He couldn't recall that he'd been dreaming, any nightmarish incident which had caused him to wake. He turned restlessly towards Max, sound asleep in the other bed. At least he supposed the other was asleep.

'Max, you awake?'

A sleepy mumble answered him. Dan raised his voice slightly. 'You awake, Max?'

Another grumble from the other bed and then Max sat up suddenly. 'Eh? What is it?'

'You awake?'

'I am now,' was the reply, with only a trace of bitterness in it. 'Whassermarrer?' Max yawned.

'Something woke me,' Dan said. 'I wondered if you'd heard it.'

'How could I, I was asleep. Emphasise *was*.'

'Sorry, old chap, if I woke you,' Dan said contritely. 'I sort of wondered if you were awake — '

'Now you know I wasn't,' Max said with commendable politeness, 'can I go to sleep again?'

'You sure you didn't hear something?'

'I wasn't awake.'

'Must have heard whatever it was in my sleep, I suppose. But now I can't remember what it was.'

'Good.' Max re-settled himself comfortably.

'It might have been a cry,' the other went on thoughtfully, 'or an owl-hoot, or a creaking board — '

'Or just that old imagination of yours.'

But Dan was still worrying over the problem. 'Or,' he said, 'the inn settling down for the night, the way these old places do.'

'I wish *you'd* settle down for the night,' Max told him, yawning ostentatiously. Adding: 'What's left of it.'

'Supposing it was a cry?' Dan suddenly sat bolt upright and said quickly: 'Max — you don't think it might be Darrell?'

'Darrell? Who's he?'

'You know. He's staying here. Makes soap.'

'Whaffor?' Max mumbled, already half asleep.

'Got a wonky heart,' Dan reminded him. 'He might have been taken ill and called out for help.'

'And,' the other muttered unfeelingly, 'he might have slipped on a piece of his silly soap and knocked himself unconscious, and,' turning on his side away from the other bed, 'I wish you'd ruddy well do the same.'

'Listen,' Dan whispered suddenly. 'A board creaked outside. I believe it was that noise woke me.'

'Now you know, you can go to sleep again.'

'I'll have to go and see. I'll only lie awake waiting for that noise again.' He swung himself out of bed. 'I won't put the light on in case it wakes you.'

'Damned decent of you.'

There was a yelp of pain as Dan caught his toe against a chair, then he found his slippers and made his way cautiously to the door. Slowly, he turned the door-handle and a dim wedge of light from the landing widened on the floor. He started to put his head outside and then with an indrawn gasp of breath, drew back as if he'd been struck and quietly closed the door again. Moving as quickly as he dared in the darkness he reached Max's bed. His voice was shaking with excitement as he bent down and whispered to where he imagined the other's ear to be.

'It *is* someone outside.'

'Who?' Max groaned and stared up at the two eyes gleaming with excitement, bent over him.

'Miss Kimber. What's that fussy little schoolteacher mooching around the place for, at this time of night?'

'Two or three reasons,' Max answered disinterestedly. 'I can think of — sleep-walking for instance.'

'People don't usually get dressed to go sleepwalking. I saw her by the light of the torch she was carrying, and I heard the swish of her raincoat.'

'In that case, she sounds as if she's taking herself for a walk. She see you?'

'Don't think so.'

Max rolled over on his side once more, muttering from his pillow: 'Perhaps she and Roberts are courting on the quiet. Don't see what it's got to do with us, anyway.'

Dan Evans stood up and began to move round to his own bed. There was, he supposed, nothing he could do about it. He got into bed and lay back staring up into the darkness. He cursed inwardly at the realisation he was going to lie awake for hours. Max stirred and he whispered across to him: 'You asleep?'

'Nearly,' came back a growl. 'I hope.'

'Doubt if I'll manage a wink.' Dan slid further down beneath the bedclothes. One thing, he reflected, about the pub, the beds were very comfortable.

After a few moments Max Mitchell twisted restlessly and sat up slowly, frowning to himself.

'Rather fancy that's given me an idea,' he said, his voice kept low. 'You seeing Miss Kimber, I mean. Why not a character in the play who walks in her sleep, and then at a crucial moment — ' He broke off and then continued: 'Or perhaps she only pretends to walk in her sleep — '

He listened to Dan's regular breathing. The blighter was sleeping like a log, Dan, who wasn't going to manage a wink.

Yes, he told himself, a sleepwalking character might be an idea. He thought it should be a spinster type. Why not like this Miss Kimber? He thought back to his idea of her only pretending to walk in her sleep. He interrupted his musing, and realised with dismay he was as wide awake as Dan had been. Could be the character, his mind rattled on, isn't really a schoolteacher, either. One of the crooks staying at the inn. Perhaps even the chief crook. Then another thought occurred to his wakening brain. Supposing she isn't even a woman, but a man disguised? Bit far-fetched, he argued critically. But he continued to mull over the idea, remembering having read somewhere how a real-life crook had impersonated a woman, and no one, not even his closest associates knew.

Suddenly he heard something which drove his thoughts out of his head. It sounded like a cry of pain. A cry from a human being. He sat bolt upright and listened carefully, every nerve tensed. Yes, there it was again. A low moan. It seemed to come from somewhere downstairs, so far as he could tell. Max turned to Dan. The other was deep in sleep. Max hesitated then got quickly out of bed He was opening the door, moving as softly as he could in his slippers. He stood listening for a repetition of the cry downstairs, and pushing his hands into his dressing-gown pockets, moved along the landing and slowly descended the stairs.

There was no further sound and he was half-way down the twisted staircase, beginning to ask himself what on earth he was doing, creeping about a strange pub looking for a cry in the night, when there came a creak above. He had paused, about to return to his warm bed, when his ears caught the sound. It was Dan, the fool, creeping after him. He called up softly, as the creaks drew nearer, 'Dan.'

'Who's that?'

It was not Dan who answered him out of the shadows, and as she spoke, Wynne Anderson paused at the top of the stairs and then came quickly and silently down. He saw she was in a dressing-gown, and glimpsed her pyjamas underneath. Her hair glinted in the gloom.

'I thought I heard a cry,' she said.

'Which is precisely what brought me out of bed.'

'I wasn't able to sleep,' she said slowly. 'And then I heard this noise.'

He wondered what it was had kept her awake. What secret sorrow had barred sleep from her? Was it some hopeless love? he wondered. He said: 'I was lying awake myself. The noise seemed to me to come from downstairs somewhere.'

'A sort of groan?'

Her corroboration that there had been some noise decided him it wasn't an overwrought imagination had caused him to hear things in the night. He recalled Dan's description of Miss Kimber in her raincoat. Could it have been the schoolteacher had been frightened by something and had cried out? He went on down the stairs, Wynne Anderson following him.

'Better not put on the lights,' she told him.

'Might attract Parry the Police?' he queried, with a quizzically raised eyebrow.

'And then that might wake everyone,' she said. 'I brought a torch, I thought it might be someone outside, in the dark.'

He took the small pocket-torch from her and they crossed the lounge, towards the passage that led off to the other part of the inn. 'It's so full of echoes, it's difficult to place where the sound could have come from,' she was saying.

'I thought it came from this direction.'

'This leads to the kitchen, and the back door. Straight ahead.'

He led the way in the darkness. He caught the faint, elusive perfume of her. The pool of light from the torch fell on the kitchen door, which was closed. He opened it and they stood in the low-ceilinged kitchen, pots and pans gleamed as the beam of light travelled round. There was no one there. They crossed to another door and he turned the key in the heavy lock, and drew the bolts.

They were in a large yard above two sides of which the mountain towered, dark and brooding, seeming to disappear into the blackness of the sky. Overhead the stars glimmered, they seemed to be very near, and a light breeze stirred eerily in the branches of a tree. In a high wall to their left, the torch-beam held another door. The girl said: 'It leads to the road. It'll be locked and bolted, too.'

The travelling pool of light flickered over something near the door and he heard her give a little gasp. Her hand clutched at his arm. 'What's that?'

The torch-beam was directed steadily on to a dark, inert shape.

The pool of light expanded, until they reached the inanimate bulging object. He prodded it with his foot and it toppled over on its side. 'Nothing more sinister than a sack of potatoes,' he said.

As she breathed a heartfelt sigh, he turned the torch on to the door in the wall. 'So long as we remember to lock up after us,' drawing the bolts and turning the key in the lock.

'I'll remind you.'

The road was empty. The light from the torch was swallowed up by the hungry darkness all around. There was no sign of anyone. From whence had the cry come? It seemed unlikely both he and the girl could have imagined it, or had mistaken some animal — a rabbit, attacked by a fox, for instance — for a human being. He felt a touch on his arm at the same time as he caught the crunch of approaching footsteps on the road.

'Somebody coming this way,' the girl whispered.

It sounded like a man. Max had switched off his torch, so it was probable whoever it was out there in the darkness imagined themselves to be alone. Max would let the oncomer draw nearer, until well within range of the torch-light.

'Don't call out,' he warned Wynne Anderson, in a low voice. He breathed in the perfume of her hair. Involuntarily, yet very conscious of what he was doing, he put his arm round her protectively. Her waist was very slim and she was soft and warm. She did not draw away.

Max switched on the torch. The approaching figure immediately halted and stood spotlighted, blinking and then raising a hand to ward the light off his face.

'Mr. Price,' the girl exclaimed.

On hearing her voice, the old man came forward. 'Miss Anderson. It's you — ?' Inevitably he sneezed.

'I thought,' Max said, 'you were leaving the car here till the morning?'

The other paused, one ear turned towards them. 'Isn't that one of the gentlemen I brought here?'

'It's Mr. Mitchell,' the girl said.

'Fancy meeting you, sir.' Max shifted the torch away from Price's face and the old man stood peering at them uncertainly.

'We couldn't think who it was, out so late,' Wynne Anderson said.

Price hesitated for a moment, as if uncertain what had been said to him. Then: 'Came along to be sure the car was all right.'

'As I remember it had broken down,' Max reminded him, 'no one's likely to run off with it.'

But the other either misheard him or chose to ignore his tone of mild sarcasm. Max shone the torch on the car which was drawn up outside the inn. It had not been spirited away. He heard Price give what might have been a satisfied grunt of recognition, but the old man made no further comment.

'You didn't happen to meet anyone?' the girl asked him.

'Meet anyone?' he echoed.

'Or hear anyone cry out?'

He regarded her from underneath his grey bristling brows and the shiny peak of his cap which was still stuck on the back of his head and which shook slowly from side to side, 'No, I didn't meet nor hear no one.' He paused, then: 'I'll be going home.'

'You don't want to be walking around with that cold of yours,' Wynne Anderson agreed. They listened to his footsteps fading into the darkness.

'His story he was seeing if his car was still here sounded pretty thin,' the girl said.

Max thought so, too, the old chap couldn't have sounded less convincing. 'Probably got a ferret in his pocket all the time.'

She glanced up at him. 'Ferret?' She gave a shudder. 'Why one of those awful things?'

'Handy when you're poaching. That's his side-line, according to your local gendarmerie.'

They stood there indecisively, staring into the darkness. Then she said: 'He doesn't seem to have been much help about our mystery voice.'

'We've struck a blank out here.'

'Perhaps it was indoors all the time.'

'We searched pretty thoroughly,' she

said, then she was alert, listening again.

Footsteps were approaching once more, but from the other direction now. Max was thinking they might as well be in Euston Station, the traffic here was so busy. The nearing footsteps were a man's also, but brisk and purposeful and at the same moment they faced the newcomer, Max and the girl were held in a sudden spotlight from a torch. A voice greeted them:

'Why, if it isn't Miss Anderson, and Mr. — er — ' Parry the Police waited to be prompted.

'The name's Mitchell.'

'Ah, yes, sir — Mr. Mitchell.' The torch-beam left their faces and in its reflection they could see his own face, shadowed by the helmet, slightly amused and quizzical. He smoothed his moustache. 'I — er — you didn't happen to notice anyone pass this way?'

Max opened his mouth to tell the other of their encounter with old Price, but was stopped by a discreet nudge from the girl, who said: 'We were just going to ask you the same question.' She turned to Max.

'Weren't we, Mr. Mitchell?'

He mumbled an affirmative reply, and she continued: 'We both thought we heard someone cry out, and met each other, by chance, downstairs. At first we thought it was indoors, but couldn't find anything — '

'So we looked out here.' Max found his voice.

'Perhaps it was a bird or some animal you heard.'

'We're beginning to think it must have been,' Wynne Anderson said. 'Though it didn't seem like it to either of us.'

Parry smoothed his moustache again thoughtfully. 'I'll keep my eyes open. Though I always do,' he said, 'and that's a fact.'

'I'm sure you do,' she said.

'What with certain people,' Parry went on darkly, 'who I won't name, creeping about of a night — ' He choked with increasing rancour. 'But just let me lay hands on the wheezing, thieving old poacher, and I'll — ' He spluttered incoherently into a cough, then said more calmly: 'Well — I'll be getting along on my beat.'

His brisk footsteps had receded along the road before the girl said to Max: 'I really didn't see why we should tell him. About Mr. Price.'

'I suppose it would have spoiled their fun.'

She gave a little shiver — she had moved out of his encircling arm earlier on — and he said: 'Feeling cold?'

'Not really.' She was staring upwards.

'Shame to go in, it's such a lovely night,' she sighed. 'Just look at those stars.'

'Marvellous,' he breathed.

Her face was upturned to him. 'You're not looking at them.'

He gave a sudden exclamation. 'Good heavens.'

'What is it?' Her brow was anxious.

'And I thought it happened only in songs or books.'

'What *is* it?'

'The stars,' he told her. 'I *can* see them in your eyes.'

There was a little pause. The wind whispered softly in the branches and stirred her hair. Her eyes were very large and soft behind the slanting horn-rims. They were not greenish hazel any more, but dark, almost deep violet.

'I think perhaps we should go in,' she said.

He followed her slowly back into the yard, bolting and locking the gate behind them. They crossed the yard and were in the kitchen, the lock turned, the bolt shot home. 'Roberts will have nothing to grouch about,' he smiled at her. But she hadn't heard him, he could glimpse her teeth gleaming between her parted lips as she raised her head in an attitude of listening to something else.

'Thought I heard that sound again,' she said. 'It seemed to come from — ' She broke off and he followed her quickly out of the kitchen.

They were in the passage leading back to the lounge, but a few yards along she suddenly turned to the left. It was a narrower passage, which he had somehow omitted to notice before. His torch flashing ahead showed a twisting flight of stairs leading up, he presumed, to a landing at the back of the inn. The stairs creaked as the girl led the way. Suddenly, she paused with a gasp.

The beam of light fell in a pool upon a great, crumpled shape, slumped head downwards where the stairs twisted sharply. 'Uncle.'

Max was beside her, staring down at the figure, so curiously contorted. He knew even as he lifted up the bearded face that Josh Jones was dead.

5

Max Mitchell crouched back from the body and took the girl's arm in a firm grip. She met his gaze and her lower lip trembled, until she bit into it. In the glow from the torch she was deathly pale, her face suddenly haggard.

'I'm afraid,' he said gently, 'it's no good. He's dead.'

'You're quite sure?'

'He must have fallen very heavily. His neck . . . '

She gave a little moan and his arm was round her, helping her to her feet. She swayed and then steadied herself. He saw the softly-rounded chin outlined by the torch-light harden, her slender body stiffened against his arm as she pulled herself together. She was taking it pretty well. 'Isn't there anything we can do?'

'I think we ought to get a doctor.' It was more to help her brace herself against the shock of what had happened by suggesting some, any sort of action, to her.

'I'll go and 'phone him.'

He would remain where he was, he told her. He found the electric-light switch. She agreed there was no reason against putting the lights on, now. It didn't matter any more. Her slippers clacked down the twisting stairs as she hurried away to telephone. Poor kid, he thought, as he regarded that sprawling figure at his feet. What a terrible smack in the face for her.

He tried to decide how Josh Jones could have plunged to his death. The stairs were twisted and narrow, dangerous enough to anyone unaware of them, but to the dead man they must have been familiar. And why had he been descending, or ascending them in the dark?

The question framing itself in his mind sent his speculations shooting off at a tangent, searching for the answer to another query which had earlier raised itself. It seemed to have little connection with the tragedy which he had now encountered, yet it had been suspended

113

back of his mind, now it swung momentarily to the forefront.

He was recalling Dan's hallucinatory discovery in room number six. His overwrought imagination which had conjured up the picture of a murderer on the run asleep in a chair in a room which then proved to be unoccupied. Unoccupied — and Roberts had previously asserted with emphasis there wasn't a room in the place available. All the time there had been at least two rooms vacant. Seven, which Roberts had suddenly remembered had been vacated the day before — and room six. Why had the dark, crafty-eyed man lied so desperately in an effort to prevent two unexpected travellers from staying the night?

Max could find no answer to the riddle. As his thoughts returned to the sudden death of the inn's owner, he heard footsteps ascending the stairs. The girl had been very quick getting on to the doctor, he was thinking, then found himself face to face with Miss Kimber.

She stood there, her indeterminately coloured hair slightly awry, her usually faded features glowing from the effects of the fresh, night air. One hand was thrust deep into her raincoat while the other pressed against the oak-panelled side of the stairs. She was breathing a trifle quickly and now, her eyes dilating at the sight of Josh Jones, a hand flew to her mouth.

'I'm afraid there's been an accident,' Max said quietly. She gasped inarticulately and he went on: 'Miss Anderson and I have just found him.'

'Dead?'

He nodded. 'He must have fallen. His neck's broken.'

She stared at the inert shape, then made some explanation of her unexpected appearance. 'I — I couldn't sleep . . . Went out for a walk, admiring the view by the moonlight — ' She burbled on and then exclaimed: 'Oh, poor man — and his niece, the shock — '

'She's taken it not too badly. 'Phoning for the doctor, now.' He saw her doubtful glance at the body. 'He can't do anything, but I thought — '

She caught on and nodded. 'Of course.

I'll go to her.' She was suddenly business-like, efficient and decisive. 'In case she may suddenly collapse,' she said turning away. The swish of her raincoat receded with her muttering: 'Sometimes happens — when the first shock's over . . .'

She wasn't walking in her sleep, he thought irrelevantly, remembering Dan's account of having seen her float past their bedroom. It was at that precise moment that Dan's voice reached him quietly from the top of the stairs.

'Max — that you?'

The other came into sight, peering down. 'I woke up and you'd gone, I got up, and thought I heard you talking — ' He broke off, his breath hissing between his teeth. 'Good God — '

He came down so quickly he almost slipped. Steadying himself against the wall he reached Max's side.

'It's the uncle,' Max said. 'Afraid he's had it.'

'Broke his neck, eh?'

'The girl and I found him.' Max was suddenly staring fixedly at the body. He said, his voice edged with suppressed excitement: 'Notice anything unusual — about his coat?'

Following the direction of his look, Dan bent to obtain a closer view. It was a double-breasted coat of grey worsted. There was something about it struck him as slightly off-key, but he couldn't quite see what it was. He frowned, and stood upright, head to one side in an effort to discern what was amiss about the coat's appearance. He gave an exclamation of comprehension as Max said in his ear: 'It's buttoned up on the *left* side.'

'Of course, it should button on the right.' Now he realised what was odd about the coat. 'It looks as if,' he said slowly, speaking his thoughts aloud, 'it'd been put on by someone else — hurriedly.'

'Does, doesn't it?'

Dan jerked round, his jaw dropping a trifle. '*After* he was dead? That what you're driving at?'

'The thought does spring to mind.'

'But — but why should anyone want to put his coat on for him after he was dead?'

Max regarded him blandly. 'Your hunch is as good as mine,' he said. 'But say, for example,' an abstract look in his eyes, 'he died before he landed down here, as he was going to bed. And someone, for some reason — perhaps they wanted him to appear as if he'd come upstairs recently, or, maybe, just because they had a tidy mind — '

'He was dead before he — ?' Dan whispered. 'But that means he was — ' His imagination boggled at the implication in the other's suggestion. 'He couldn't have been. It's an accident.'

'I said that your hunch — '

'Max,' the other's voice was low and harsh, 'what are you getting at — ?'

'Forget it for now,' Max said abruptly, ear turned towards the passage below, 'someone's coming.'

It was Miss Kimber. As Dan regarded her with surprise Max explained quickly: 'Miss Kimber couldn't sleep, and has just come in from a walk.'

Dan blinked at him, then at the schoolmistress who was saying to Max: 'The doctor's on his way. Poor thing, she was beginning to break down — she's gone to her room.'

'Dreadful business for her,' Dan said.

She nodded somewhat absently. 'I'm going along to see if she'll let me give her a sedative.'

'We'll wait around for the doctor,' Max said.

She made a move up the stairs, then averting her head from the body, stepped back. 'I — I think I won't go this way,' she murmured half apologetically, 'I'll use the other stairs.'

'Funny old girl,' Dan said after she'd gone.

'Will you wait here? While I nip along — '

'Of course, old chap,' Dan said easily. 'You go and see how she is.'

Max gave him a glance, but the other's expression appeared innocent enough. 'It's the local cop I want to get hold of. He might be passing on his beat again.'

'Police? You seriously think that — ?' He seemed only half convinced by the other's theory. 'What'll you tell him?'

'You see, another explanation for the

poor devil's coat being buttoned wrongly has just struck me.'

'What is it?'

'Women's coats,' Max said, 'always do up on the left-hand side.'

'You mean a woman might have buttoned it? In other words — ' His puzzlement was profound. 'But who — you don't suspect Miss Kimber?'

He looked even more bewildered at the reply: 'That's for our pal Parry to work on.' Max started down the stairs. 'I'll be as quick as I can.'

'Max . . . '

Max Mitchell halted at the tone in the other's voice. Dan came slowly down to join him. 'Before you rush off,' he said slowly, 'don't you think — well — I was going to suggest you slept on it.'

'You think I'm the one who's imagining things now?'

Dan smiled back at him, a rueful smile. 'I did get a bit excited over Vernon — and you persuaded me I was seeing things.'

Max wondered if the other had been imagining things after all. But he did not give expression to his thoughts. At the same time he had to admit he himself was now giving rein to hasty judgment. He didn't want to make a fool of himself, of course. Perhaps Dan's advice was the most sensible. Sleep on it, and see how it looked with the few remaining hours of night to give the problem perspective.

'You may be right,' he said.

'The doctor will be here any minute. I dare say he'll call in the cops as a matter of routine, it being sudden death and all that.'

That was true, Max reflected. It might be wise to await the medical verdict. The doctor need know nothing about any suspicions regarding the circumstances of Josh Jones' death. He said as much to Dan.

'In the morning,' the latter said, 'if you still feel convinced there's something nasty in the woodshed, we'll pop along and tell all to Parry.'

'I'll settle for that,' Max said.

They heard a knocking on the front door, then the sound of the door being opened and Roberts' and another man's voice. No doubt it was the doctor, and

Roberts, aroused by Miss Kimber and informed of what had happened, had come down in time to admit him.

Dan and Max got back to their room about half an hour later, leaving Roberts to wait up for the ambulance, which was expected to arrive. at any moment to remove the dead man. Max had obtained a glimpse of the girl, looking very white and shaken, with Miss Kimber and the doctor in attendance.

He and Dan heard the ambulance arrive as they returned to bed. It drove away presently, the front door closed and the Crooked Inn settled down once more for the night. Max and Dan did not wake again until a knocking and Roberts' voice outside their door warned them it was time to get up. Dan was listening to Roberts' footsteps descending the stairs. Then Max was out of bed, pulling on his dressing-gown, and he followed suit.

In between their trips to the bathroom and pauses for shaving they discussed last night's events in carefully subdued tones. As a result of casually put questions to Dr. Griffiths, Max had ascertained that he appeared satisfied Josh Jones had accidentally slipped and broken his neck. Nevertheless the doctor considered it his duty to advise the police of the tragedy, leaving it for them to decide whether or not an inquest was necessary.

Max felt reasonably certain Dr. Griffiths had no suspicion of there being any element of foul play. 'Unless I'm much mistaken,' Max told Dan, 'the inquest, if any, will bring in a verdict in line with the doctor's opinion.'

'Question therefore is,' Dan knotted his tie, scrutinised it critically in the mirror and decided to unknot and re-tie it, 'should we throw a spanner in the works? Or,' standing back to regard the tie more approvingly now, 'do we let sleeping dogs lie?'

'As I see it,' Max said, pausing to stare out of the window at the sunlit road and then turning away thoughtfully, 'the question is something else.' In answer to the other's look, he explained. 'If we do go to the police with our suspicions what have we got to lose? We, or, if we've jumped to wrong conclusions, anyone else for that matter?'

Dan agreed if no one was guilty no one would suffer as a result of Josh Jones' death being discreetly investigated further. And they could shake the dust of Mynydd Llanberis off their feet with no uncomfortable feeling they'd shirked acting upon the courage of their convictions. They wouldn't be dogged by the possibility that due to their timidity and unconcern a murder had gone undetected and unpunished.

'Of course,' Dan said, 'I'm forced to admit that getting our ideas off our chests to that Parry character intrigues me from another angle.'

'You mean, as a source of material which we may be able to work into the play?'

'Even if we make the most awful chumps of ourselves at least we'll get something for our money. And after all,' a further thought striking him, 'Parry's suspicions regarding us — that one of us might be a killer on the run — were aroused on a much flimsier excuse.'

The aroma of bacon and cooking

began to pervade the room and Dan sniffed appreciatively. He finished dressing and stood waiting at the door. Max tied a shoe-lace and stood up, his long, thin face clouded. The events of last night paraded before his mind's eye in swift succession. Standing out like towers of suspicion were, he mentally ticked off, Roberts' desperately lying efforts to prevent their staying the night, Dan's vision of the sleeping murderer — if vision it was — and the strange circumstances of Josh Jones' death: the fact that anyone so familiar with the treacherously twisting staircase would descend it in the dark, plus the significance of the wrongly-buttoned coat.

He glanced at Dan. 'What's the decision?'

The other sniffed hungrily at the increasingly appetising aroma of breakfast awaiting them. 'I'm on your side,' he said. 'Let's look in on Parry. At least for our art's sake, if for nothing else.'

They went down to breakfast.

Roberts served them in an automaton-like manner, his dark features haggard and mournful, his eyes veiled, his answers to every question monosyllabic. Max and Dan were the only ones at breakfast. Miss Kimber had not yet put in an appearance and neither had the girl. Mr. Darrell had, as usual, breakfasted an hour before and had left for the river. Even the proximity of a sudden tragedy could not, it seemed, keep him from his fishing.

Max and Dan ate their breakfast hungrily and speedily, anxious to catch Parry at home in case the latter's duties took him out early. The morning was bright and warm, and as they set out in the direction of the village, where they imagined the policeman was to be found, they took great gulps of sweet mountain air. It seemed impossible to believe that a stark tragedy could stalk through such peace and gentle beauty. To their right as they unobtrusively quitted the inn and headed down the tree-shaded road, the Crooked Mountain climbed and twisted majestically against the blue sky. Sheep dotted the rising slopes in white, slowly-moving blobs.

To their left undulating fields ran away

to a long, low wooded ridge. Cattle grazed quietly along the edge of what from the road seemed to be a fairly wide stream which pushed its way towards the beginning of a blue-hazed valley way ahead. A man, accompanied by a sheep-dog, its black and white coat catching the sunlight, passed through a gate and disappeared behind a small copse. The only sounds were the distant mutter of sheep, birds singing in the hedges and the crunch of their own shoes on the road.

They walked swiftly, Max chewing appreciatively on his pipe, Dan finishing an after-breakfast cigarette. The sound of their footsteps deflected Max's thoughts to last night. He and Wynne Anderson, hearing first old Price and then Parry approach out of the darkness. He was remembering the soft warmth of her, the scent of her hair. There was little he could do to help her now, he told himself. Miss Kimber was the one to whom the girl would turn in her grief. No doubt, too, he reflected, Roberts for all his faults and saturnine exterior, would do his best to help the niece of his late employer.

They made no attempt to ask the whereabouts of the police station from the people of the village who passed with their friendly smiles and greetings. Mynydd Llanberis consisted of only a few straggling cottages, snugly built of local stone with their slate roofs and neat porches. Inevitably the house, with its easily recognisable sign, denoting its special significance in that quiet spot must come into view. There it was now, a detached, somewhat modern-looking house in a small garden, bounded on one side by a grey, stucco-walled chapel and on the other by farm buildings. Max and Dan paused outside the gate to make sure they were not observed by any curious villagers. They went up the little garden path, with its carefully tended flower-beds on either side.

The door was opened by Parry the Police himself.

Some half an hour later Parry knocked the dottle out of his pipe into a large ash-tray at his elbow, leaned back in his chair, eyed first Max and then Dan. 'I'm telling you two gentlemen I'm very glad you've come along, and that's a fact.'

They were sitting in the front room which had been converted into the police station's one office, its distempered walls adorned with a miscellany of official notices ranging from those concerning the Colorado Beetle and foot-and-mouth warnings to a notice bearing a familiar photograph beneath the legend: WANTED FOR MURDER. Behind Parry was a high sloping desk, on which were neatly arranged various forms and documents, copies of police journals, a large metal inkstand, holding two or three pens and an old-fashioned type telephone. On a peg behind the door hung a dark blue cape and Parry's helmet.

P.C. Parry drained the cup of tea — his sister, a gipsy-visaged woman, who kept house for him, the policeman was a confirmed bachelor, had brought in tea for the three of them. He pushed his chair back and crossed to the fireplace, over which hung an enlarged photograph of himself resplendent in the uniform of a World War II soldier. He filled his pipe

129

from a tin of tobacco and bracing himself against the mantelpiece, said: 'Nothing's been lost by waiting until this morning, you needn't let that worry you.'

'I persuaded Mr. Mitchell to sleep on it.'

'And a lot of trouble would be spared the world,' the other said, 'if only more people slept first before jumping in and acting on their mad ideas without due consideration. Dr. Griffiths being satisfied it was an accident, the deceased was removed, but no matter.'

He tamped down the tobacco in the black, charred bowl and applied a match to it. The room began to fill with the fumes of strong shag as Dan asked:

'There may be something in it then?'

Parry took the pipe from under his ragged moustache and succeeded in assuming a non-committal expression. 'Enough for me to get on to my sergeant at Llanberis.'

'You think poor old Josh Jones didn't fall, but might have been pushed?'

'We won't go so far as that, Mr. Mitchell. No, we won't go so far as that.

We'll merely say the circumstances of his death, as very helpfully brought to my notice by you gentlemen, appear to warrant' — he paused before concluding judiciously — 'further investigation.'

'Quite,' Dan contrived to restrain himself from giving Max a wink.

Parry the Police was saying: 'I believe I've got the main point of both your stories.' He glanced at Dan. 'Beginning with you seeing him' — he jerked a thumb at the photo on the wall — 'asleep in that room and deciding you were mistaken — '

'And it was him all the time.'

Parry contemplated his pipe for a moment. 'There's no news of his capture, so far, that's true,' was all he would admit. 'We have no *proof* it was him. You still might have been mistaken.'

'But surely,' Dan argued, 'if the uncle *was* murdered, Vernon did it? And that blighter Roberts knew he was there all along?'

'Whether it was murder and if so who committed it is no more than surmise at the moment. However . . . later you were awakened by a noise and saw this Miss Kimber pass your room?'

'After which,' Dan Evans said, 'I went off to sleep and left the rest of the plot to my friend.'

Parry's expression grew a trifle pained at the flippant note in the other's tone, and Max threw Dan a warning glance. The policeman had regarded their visit in all seriousness. It was only fair to him in return not to treat the tragic business at the Crooked Inn as if it were no more than the basis of a stage play. Even if, in fact, it might prove extremely useful from that point of view. Parry turned to Max.

'And you, Mr. Mitchell, hearing this cry, got up to try and ascertain the cause of same. As a result you met the deceased's niece and continued the search with her?'

'Leaving out the trimmings, that's about it.'

'As to the trimmings,' the other said with an unexpected hint of dry humour twinkling in his eyes, 'we'll tack them on in due course.' He pushed himself off the mantelpiece and moved over to the desk.

'I'll give Llanberis a ring.'

They watched him pick up the receiver off its hook. He was about to speak into it, smoothing his moustache thoughtfully, when he apparently changed his mind and hung up. He met the others' quizzical expressions.

'The line might get crossed. In which case the wrong person might overhear what I was saying to Sergeant Morris. Which wouldn't do at all, and that's a fact.' He went on: 'I'll go over and see him.' He glanced at the wall-clock. It was twenty minutes past nine.

'Like us to come with you?' Max offered.

The other watched a ring of tobacco-smoke shiver on the air, then expand and then disintegrate before he replied. 'It would be very helpful of you.'

'Only too glad,' Dan said. Max glanced at him and smiled inwardly. He knew Dan's eagerness to make the acquaintance of the Llanberis police was prompted less by a desire to be helpful than his incorrigible hope of obtaining more material to incorporate in the play. 'We have to let the Criccieth Arms know we shan't be wanting their room tonight, either.'

Max's look turned to one of surprise. 'Shan't we?'

'We must settle up with them for all the trouble we've caused.'

'Where, just as a matter of interest, are we going to stay?'

It was the other's turn to appear surprised. 'Right where we stayed last night,' he said. 'The Crooked Inn.'

'Oh . . . ' Max shrugged. There was no doubt Dan, in pursuance of his craft was determined to extract every particle of dramatic value possible out of the mysterious situation in which they had been inadvertently plunged. Max dismissed a sudden qualm that the other's enthusiasm might push him too far in an attempt to precipitate further exciting incidents. He felt Dan was inclined to be somewhat incalculable in his less restrained moments.

'I'm sure your co-operation will be very much appreciated,' Parry the Police was saying. 'I'll obtain a car from Llanberis to fetch us.'

'Ready when you are,' Dan said.

'I think we'd better get back to the inn first,' Max said, 'for a word with the niece. To fix up about our staying on.'

Dan agreed, then said: 'She may want to close up the place.'

'That had occurred to me,' Max said.

Parry gave a cough. 'You won't let out a hint we suspect her uncle's death may be anything other than an unfortunate accident? Not even to the poor young woman? In case we are barking up the wrong tree.'

'Trust us,' Dan said.

There was a pause, while P.C. Parry seemed absorbed in his pipe. The other two got to their feet and made as if to set off back to the inn. The policeman bestirred himself and then without looking up queried slowly: 'Miss Kimber . . . . Schoolteacher, isn't she?'

'She did say something about being one,' Dan said and Max gave a confirmatory nod.

'School at — where was it — ?' Max began, but saw that Parry did not appear very interested. He was muttering half to himself.

'Wonder if it's that brings her to a quiet spot like Mynydd Llanberis for her holiday?'

Dan regarded him with a slightly corrugated brow. 'Afraid I don't quite see what she's got to do with — with — ' his puzzlement tapered off.

The other clamped his teeth over his pipe-stem, expelled a cloud of smoke, removed his pipe again and went on. 'I can imagine her pupils leading her quite a dance, and that's a fact. Her not being very observant.'

'How do you know she's not observant?' Max was impelled to inquire.

Parry the Police allowed a faint, good-humoured flicker to play about the ends of his moustache. 'One of the frills you mentioned,' he said slowly. 'Which have got to be tacked on.' He prodded at the other with his pipe. 'When she came in last night and found you with the — er — late Mr. Jones, didn't you say she referred to having been out for a walk?'

'She did.'

'In the moonlight.'

'Yes . . . '

'You yourself had not long come in with Miss Anderson,' Parry said. He paused before asking innocently: 'Did you remember any moon?'

Max's mind filled with the picture of those large eyes behind the slanted, almond-shaped glasses, the stars reflected in their depths. He sensed Dan's glance fixed on him as he said:

'There wasn't any moon.'

6

Max and Dan had hurried back through the village and were half-way along the road to the inn, when they were halted by a sudden shout just behind them. They turned to see Darrell climb over a gate leading out of the fields stretching away towards the river. He caught up with them, clutching what seemed to be an armful of rods in their cases, with haversacks hanging all over him, and so many fly-hooks stuck on his hat and sports-jacket he looked as if a minor swarm of insects had settled upon him.

'Any luck?' Dan asked conversationally as the other approached them, a little breathless.

Darrell pulled a sour face. 'I'm moving to another part of the stream,' he said. 'Not a nibble in that part,' with a backward jerk of his head. His plump features clouded over as he said: 'Dreadful about Josh Jones.' Max and Dan made appropriate answers and the other went on. 'Seems I was the only one who slept through it. Couldn't credit it when Roberts told me this morning. And the poor girl. Only relative, Roberts says. By the way,' he rattled, 'think they'll have to close up the inn? At any rate until a new landlord takes over?'

'Perhaps Roberts'll keep it going,' Dan said.

'That's an idea.' Then the thought seemed to cause him to frown. 'Not exactly a little ray of sunshine, and between you and me I'm sure he's secretly wallowing in the tragedy. All the same,' he admitted reluctantly, 'he's competent enough.'

'I'm sure he is,' Dan said.

'Dear, oh, dear,' the other sighed gustily. 'How slender the thread that suspends us between this life and the next.'

Max and Dan glanced at each other. They were remembering Darrell's gasps for breath the night before and his disclosure his heart wasn't all it might be. Dan mumbled something.

'Ah, well,' the other brightened, 'I suppose I'd better see how the damned trout are behaving further along.' He gave them a speculative look. 'I suppose you'll make use of this incident in one of your plays, eh? Must be all grist that comes to your mill. You'll be gone when I return, so I'll say good-bye to you now. Very interesting to have met you.'

They watched him for a moment march briskly down the road, and then continued on their way. Arriving at the inn they found Roberts hovering about in the lounge. In answer to Max's query the man, in shirt-sleeves and green baize apron, replied that Wynne Anderson was upstairs. 'Doctor's with her,' he said, his attitude somewhat more expansive than it had been at breakfast. 'Anything I can do?'

Max said he would wait in the lounge till the doctor had gone. Roberts still hovered around indecisively, not unlike some nervous jackdaw. Dan said he looked as if he'd had a bad night, whereupon Roberts pounced on what was obviously the opportunity he'd been awaiting to unburden his heart.

'I had a premonition something was going to happen,' he said, advancing closer, his dark eyes flashing fanatically.

'Premonition?' Dan was ready to listen to what the man had to say in the hope of him revealing something of greater significance than he might intend.

'The Crooked Inn's an odd place, sir. That's why I tried to put you off staying here last night.'

Max gave him a look and said dryly: 'Very thoughtful of you.'

'I was right too, you must admit that — after what's happened.' The others said nothing and Roberts proceeded, heedless of whether he received encouragement, or not. 'Most people don't sense anything, but this place breathes evil. Like some dark, twisted animal it reminds me of, lying in wait.'

'I must say,' Max was slightly amused by the other's rhetoric, 'it doesn't strike me altogether like that.'

'Ah,' Roberts cried, pointing a dramatic finger at Dan, 'but this gentleman sensed it, didn't he? The ghost you saw, sir

— that awful figure you mistook for that murderer who's roaming about.'

'We put that down to my slightly over-active brain.'

'Believe me, sir,' Roberts lowered his voice dramatically, 'though I didn't say so, I knew death was about to walk.'

He gave a glance over his shoulder as if to make sure he was in no danger of being overheard. Edging closer, he told them hoarsely: 'I could hear the inn whispering, like it does at night — whispering black wickedness.'

'You believe some supernatural force caused Mr. Jones' death?' Max asked.

The other nodded vigorously. 'Oh, it's no good telling Parry the Police. Only laugh at me. And the doctor — '

He broke off. As the others followed his glance there was a movement on the stairs and the sparse figure of Dr. Griffiths descended. He bade them good-morning and they heard his car start up and drive off. Max turned to Roberts.

'Sorry not to be able to hear more about your theory. Some other time.'

'No theory, sir, it's a proved fact . . . ' Roberts gave a long-suffering shrug. 'But you only think I'm a bit gone in my senses. I'll go and tell Miss Anderson you're here.'

Max and Dan waited in silence for his reappearance. The latter had already suggested it wasn't necessary for them both to see the girl, who'd be in little mood for talking to comparative strangers. As Max had got to know her rather the better he should see her now.

Roberts came downstairs. 'Miss Anderson says for you to come up, sir.'

She was at the window in her room which was furnished like a bed-sitting-room, small writing-desk in one corner and two comfortable armchairs. She moved from the window, her hair turning to a deep red as it escaped a beam of sunlight.

'I just wanted to — ' Max broke off and blurted out: 'You poor kid.'

'I'm beginning to pick up the pieces,' she said in a low voice. 'Dr. Griffiths is being wonderfully kind and Miss Kimber . . . '

'I'm glad. Look,' after a moment, 'I don't want to butt in — I mean, I'm sure you've made all your plans, but what are you going to do?'

She would remain at the inn, she told him. Until after the funeral at any rate. Then a solicitor friend of Dr. Griffiths from Caernarvon would advise her about everything. She was Josh Jones' only relative, there was no one else.

'I see — Wynne,' he said. 'You can call me Max, if you can bear it.'

She gave him a shaky little laugh. 'I'll try.'

'I'd like you to let me stick by you. Until everything does get straightened out a bit for you.'

'You don't have to worry about me.'

'I know I don't have to,' he said. 'But can I?'

She looked up at him, her face still deathly pale, her eyes troubled. For a moment she seemed to be considering whether she would not rather face up to her troubles on her own. A chill touched his heart. Then she said:

'You're very kind.'

'You never know,' his spirits rising, 'I might come in useful.'

'You've got your work,' she began, but he interrupted her.

'If the room isn't wanted for anyone, then Dan and I will stay on for a couple of days.'

'You're sure you wouldn't both be more comfortable at Llanberis?'

He glanced at his watch. 'We're just going over there — to put things right with the Criccieth Arms. Be back after lunch.'

He found Dan awaiting him in the lounge. They did not notice Roberts watching them as they went out.

Roberts stood at the door staring after them with a hooded expression in his eyes. With a glance at the car still where it had been left last night and awaiting old Price to return for it, he moved away and glanced up in the direction of Wynne Anderson's room. He moved towards the passage with a swift, cat-like movement.

Half-way along the passage was the shallow curtained recess where the 'phone-extension, also the old-fashioned type, stood on a shelf, a local directory suspended from a hook. He paused for a moment, listening, then came back to glance into the lounge as if to make sure no one was about.

At that moment the telephone-extension rang.

Meanwhile, oblivious that their departure from the inn had been the object of Roberts' speculative scrutiny, Dan and Max were half-way through the village. As they turned a bend in a row of cottages the former gave an exclamation.

'Miss Kimber . . . '

Sure enough it was the schoolteacher emerging from a telephone-kiosk at the side of the road. She was proceeding along the road away from them when another familiar figure stood in her path, touching his cap with a friendly smile. It was old Price, carrying a petrol-can.

The two chatted together for a few moments and then as Dan and Max drew within twenty or thirty yards of them, Miss Kimber hurried on, leaving Price looking back after her, his cap raised. The retreating Miss Kimber had by now broken into a short run. Then she disappeared behind the huge trunk of a tree which leaned precariously over to mask a corner in the road. Old Price turned and approached Dan and Max, his face breaking into a welcoming smile as he recognised them. As they reached him he halted and gave an inevitable sneeze.

'You ought to have stayed in bed, last night, instead of being so concerned about your — er — car.'

But Price failed to catch or chose to ignore the gibe in Max's tone. He indicated the petrol-can. 'On my way to fetch it from the inn, now, I am. But what a sad happening there last night.' He shook his head. 'Poor girl,' he continued. 'I was saying to Miss Kimber — '

Dan said: 'That was Miss Kimber running off like a startled hare?'

'Yes, sir. In a hurry to catch a bus.'

'Bet she broke the spinsters' hundred yards record with that dash.'

'Very active she is, sir.' The old chap turned to Max: 'Wouldn't think it, sir, to look at her.'

'You wouldn't,' Max said.

Price stifled another sneeze before it got a real grip of him and mumbling apologetically through a large, vari-hued handkerchief blew his nose.

'Better take care of that cold,' Dan warned him, 'before it takes care of you.'

Old Price nodded and shuffled off, clutching his petrol-tin. He did not glance back at the two others who watched him for a moment before they pursued their own way. Price trudged on in the direction of the inn, pausing occasionally to give a sneeze or change the can over from one hand to the other. He found the weight caused the sharp edge of the handle to cut into his fingers.

The car was there outside the inn, as he had last seen it in the early hours of the morning. He put the can down with a sigh of relief and stood beside the petrol-tank, rubbing the inside of his fingers which were cramped and stiff with rheumatism combined with the effects of the sharp handle-edge. He began to wrestle with the petrol-tank cap. It refused to budge beneath his stiff fingers and he stood up defeated. He'd better find Roberts, he decided. Roberts could get the thing off.

He shuffled to the front door of the inn and stood there peering into the lounge. He could hear light footsteps and he called out: 'Roberts . . . You there?' He kept his voice low.

'Who's that?' Wynne Anderson called, pausing halfway down the stairs. For a moment she could not make out who it was, she could see only a familiar silhouette in the doorway. Then she heard a strangled gasp.

'Who — ?' Old Price's jaw sagged and he froze. 'No, no it can't be — '

Wynne saw who it was and she came towards him. 'Oh, it's you, Mr. Price — '

But he was backing away from her, terrified, a gnarled hand thrust out as if trying to ward her off. She paused, her horn-rims fixed on him. He had gone a ghastly colour and was making strange choking sounds in his throat. Startled she heard him croak: 'It must be your ghost — '

'Ghost? What's wrong, Mr. Price?'

Something in the quietness of her

voice, the bewilderment in her manner caused him to stare at her again. His breathing grew more easy, his attitude relaxed. 'Miss Kimber,' he muttered, 'I met her in the village — she told me you were dead. Last night — '

'It was my uncle.'

'Oh, dear, I must have misheard. It's this cold of mine. Oh, Miss Anderson, I'm so sorry. Sorry to hear it was poor Mr. Josh Jones — ' He floundered again. 'I mean I'm glad it isn't you, after all, but I'm sorry all the same about your poor uncle.'

In answer to his queries she gave him an account of how the tragedy had happened, how her uncle, on his way upstairs to bed, had slipped and fallen. Then Roberts appeared and Price remembered what he had wanted to find him for. Wynne told Roberts she was going for a breath of fresh air. The two of them watched her, walking slowly, until she was out of sight. Price turned to Roberts with a great sigh.

'Fancy such a thing happening to Josh Jones,' he said. 'Big, strong man and all he was.' He shook his head and then led Roberts out to the car. The latter surveyed the vehicle with a sardonic air.

'Nothing about this junk-heap could work all right,' he observed. 'Best thing you can do is hitch a horse to it. *Might* go then.' Price protested about this defamation of the car's character, while Roberts struggled to unscrew the cap from the tank. 'Your son solder the darn thing on?' his face dark red with the effort. Then the cap shifted beneath an extra pressure of his strong, bony fingers and he unscrewed it.

He watched while the old man began pouring the petrol into the tank. Suddenly Price stopped with a little exclamation. He held the can so that the petrol dribbled into a little pool at his feet as he screwed up his eyes thoughtfully.

'What's wrong now? Engine fall out when I got the cap off?' Roberts pretended to look under the car as if to see if its insides were strewn on the road.

'But Mr. Roberts — I don't understand it.'

'Or has a dog run off with the wheel?'

151

Roberts straightened himself and jeered at the other, whose preoccupied stare was still fixed unseeingly before him.

But the other wasn't listening. 'I saw him,' he muttered. 'No doubt of it. I saw him.'

'Stop mumbling,' Roberts snapped at him, 'and get moving. This heap of old iron don't exactly ornament the scene.'

Price turned to him slowly. Then he glanced at the petrol-can he was still clutching and began to pour its remaining contents into the tank. 'I've remembered something. About Mr. Jones, it is.'

Roberts was regarding him with a pitying look as he emptied the can and then put it down. 'Mr. Jones?' he said, disinterestedly. Automatically he replaced the cap on the tank for the old man.

'It's to do with his death.'

Roberts gave the cap an extra twist and stood up, his back to the other. He pivoted round very slowly, face expressionless, his tone casual. 'What are you dithering about now?'

'You see, last night or early this morning it was really — I was out.' He broke off and then added by way of explanation: 'I was taking a little walk.'

'Out looking for a juicy rabbit, you mean.'

'And,' Price chose not to hear the other's gibe, 'I thought I'd come this way and see if the car was all right — '

'That's another good one. No one *would* move it, if they could.'

'Listen, Mr. Roberts,' the old man edged closer, a hand thrust out to grip the other's arm pleadingly. 'Please listen . . . ' He drew a deep, wheezing breath. 'It was about twenty minutes before I met Miss Anderson and one of the gentlemen I'd brought here — '

'That Mitchell chap? That must have been just before they found him dead.' An enigmatic look flickered across his face and was gone as he pounced on the other: 'So *you* were sneaking around at that time, too.'

'I'd been walking very slowly. You know how you listen to noises at night — '

'And you too deaf to hear what people are telling you half the time. Yes, go on.'

'I'd be fifty yards or so away when I

saw a light switched on here — Mr. Jones' window it was, I saw him take his coat off. He was untying his tie and then he turned, as if someone else had come into the room.'

Roberts had been lighting a stub of cigarette he had taken from behind his ear. His hand was trembling only very slightly as he asked softly: 'You saw who it was, of course?'

'I didn't,' Price said. 'They drew the curtains too quick.'

'You *didn't* see — ' Roberts only just checked himself. Instead he asked coolly: 'You didn't see who it was?'

'But the thing is ... ' Price was frowning to himself, scratching his chin with a petrol-stained forefinger, 'Miss Anderson told me — ' He began again. 'She told me — I daresay she mentioned it to you — how her uncle was *coming up to bed* when he fell downstairs.'

'I do believe I follow how your mind's working.'

Price flicked a puzzled look at him, as if he wasn't sure whether or no Roberts was being sarcastic at his expense, before he plodded on. 'Yet I saw him *after* he'd come upstairs and he was *alive*.'

'You're certain it was him?'

'No mistake. Even from where I was. Stood out clear as you do now. Big shoulders, black beard.'

'You'd swear to it, in fact?'

'On my dying oath.'

The other stared at him for a moment. Then thoughtfully, as if talking to himself he said: 'You may have given me an idea.'

'Eh?' Price frowned at him, afraid he'd missed something that had been said. Roberts remained meditatively silent and Price continued: 'Doesn't it strike you as queer?'

Roberts hunched his shoulders in a non-committal shrug. 'Seems his niece was mistaken, I agree.'

'What do you suggest we ought to do about it?'

Roberts drew his lips together judiciously. 'Don't know quite. What do *you* suggest?'

The old man blinked at him, surprised and not a little flattered at this unexpected invitation for his opinion. He spluttered for a moment or two, out of his depth. 'Don't you think — ? Well, shouldn't we tell someone? Miss Anderson? Or the doctor? Or — or — '

'The police?' Roberts prompted him gently.

Price could not help repressing a slight start of alarm. 'Police? Parry, you mean?' shifting from one foot to the other.

'He's already been along, you know.' Roberts regarded his charred cigarette-stub with apparent intent. 'Routine, of course. Case of sudden death.'

The other felt his mouth go a trifle dry. 'I hadn't thought of . . . that is — '

'Supposing you speak to Miss Anderson about it, first? What you've told me and see what she says.'

The other grabbed at the suggestion gratefully. 'That would be best, I'm sure.'

'She'd appreciate your telling her before you chatted to anyone else — '

'I won't breathe a word to no one else. I only told you because it came over me, sudden-like.'

Roberts gave him a friendly pat on the shoulder. 'Very glad you did blurt it out. Very glad.'

'When had I better see Miss Anderson?'

The other thought for a moment. 'How about coming back this afternoon?' he said. 'Say, about three-thirty.'

'I'll be here.'

'Be watching out for you. Meanwhile I'll tell — er — Miss Anderson, so she'll be expecting you. Without saying what you want to see her for, of course.'

'Fine, Mr. Roberts.'

'Until then, you'll keep all this under your hat.' It was more of a veiled threat than a question, but Price was so thankful to have dodged meeting Parry the Police he did not notice Roberts' tone. He nodded vigorously as the other went on. 'No one wants to find themselves mixed up with the police, if they can help it.'

Price ran his tongue along his dry lips. 'Parry isn't exactly a friend of mine.'

'There you are, you see.' Roberts' voice became almost jovial. 'And before you know what, finding yourself over at Llanberis answering a lot of questions.'

'Upsetting, it would be.' Price turned to the car again and picked up the

157

petrol-can. He was about to make some remark when he gave a little exclamation. 'That's funny.'

'What is?'

Price gave a faint chuckle. 'Taken my mind off of my cold. Cured it, you might say, making me forget to sneeze.'

'I'm sure that won't bother you any more.' Roberts spat the soggy cigarette-stub into the road and ground it into the dirt beneath his heel.

7

'Until you spotted that Jones' coat was wrongly buttoned up, what did you think had happened?' They were in an office at Llanberis Police Station. Dan Evans, Parry the Police and Sergeant Morris, a big, raw-boned man with a deceptively genial manner. He was leaning forward slightly as he put the question to Max.

Max glanced at Dan, then back at the sergeant.

'I thought it was an accident, I suppose,' he said.

'I'm not saying it *wasn't* an accident.' The other gave Parry a sidelong look which was acknowledged with a nod.

'It's been made pretty clear to us it doesn't do to jump to conclusions,' Dan said.

Morris nodded approvingly towards Parry. 'He's quite right to tread carefully in such a matter.'

The other preened himself. 'Clues — so-called — can lead you right up the garden,' he said. 'And that's a fact.'

'As dealers in fiction,' Sergeant Morris turned from Dan to Max, 'you'll appreciate that real-life crime isn't always so simple.'

'As dealers in real-life,' Dan said, 'you'll appreciate crime in fiction isn't always so simple either.'

The two policemen joined in a chuckle and then Morris said: 'He could have done his coat up the wrong way himself, for instance. I mean,' in explanation, 'you didn't see him come in — perhaps he'd had a drink or two — '

But his development of this line of argument was interrupted by Parry, who declared emphatically: 'I never saw or heard of Josh Jones being the worse for liquor.'

'If he was,' Max said, 'the post-mortem will show.'

Sergeant Morris threw him a look, and compressed his lips thoughtfully. 'The p.m. will do that, all right.'

'And perhaps what actually killed him,'

Dan said. 'If it was dirty work at the cross-roads.'

Silence in the bare, frugally-furnished room. The sunlight streaming in through the big windows and reflected back by the cream-distempered walls. The dark mahogany table, round which the four of them sat, gleamed. From the street the sounds of traffic passing through Llanberis, a bus rumbling past, so that the windows shook. While from the other side of the door could be heard a policeman's dull tread along the passage.

Sergeant Morris had listened to Parry's story, accompanied as it had been by corroboratory interjections from Dan and Max, with interest. When it was ended he had expressed his thanks to the latter for the trouble they had taken in coming over. He had enthused over the beautiful views of moor and mountain to be seen on the road from Mynydd Llanberis, then started putting a succession of questions to them. Now he was murmuring half to himself:

'Doctor said his neck was broken.'

Parry gave an affirmative grunt.

'Which doesn't prove, however, he wasn't dead before,' the other continued. 'Might have been poisoned or hit over the head.'

'Vernon used his bare hands, didn't he?' Parry reminded him. 'The job he did, I mean. Manual strangulation.'

'Vernon?' Sergeant Morris nodded thoughtfully. He turned to Dan. 'Talking of Vernon, you're convinced now it was him in the room, after all?'

'Yes, I am.'

'Though at the time you were persuaded you'd made a mistake?' The sergeant glanced at Max, then back to Dan.

'It seemed so nightmarish,' Dan said. 'Even now, it still sounds fantastic.'

'And Miss Anderson,' the other shifted his flat, grey eyes to Max again. 'Roaming the place at that hour — it doesn't strike you as odd?'

Max returned his gaze levelly, though there was a chill feeling at his stomach. What was this smart Welsh cop after? The way he'd put that question about Wynne — he didn't like the subtle suggestion in his voice. Surely to God he couldn't think she was anything to do with her uncle's death?

'She happened to be awake, and heard the same cry I'd heard.'

'Quite,' Sergeant Morris said. He turned to Dan, who put in with a smile:

'No odder than admiring a moon that wasn't there.'

It was Parry's turn to grin again as Sergeant Morris agreed. 'I suppose not,' he said, then to Max: 'Is she — er — attractive?'

'Not madly,' Dan said.

Max frowned at him. 'Miss Anderson,' Morris said, carefully, 'that is, not Miss Kimber.'

'Oh,' Dan looked at Max. 'She *is* rather pretty. Eh?'

The sergeant had apparently lost interest in the subject. 'Pity the doctor moved the body,' he said. 'And took the coat off.'

Parry the Police grimaced. 'He had no idea it was anything but an accident,' he said. His tone was only slightly defensive.

'And still has no idea,' Dan said. 'We

didn't mention a thing to him at all.'

'We hoped we were doing the right thing,' Max said.

Sergeant Morris asked him casually: 'You also kept quiet about it to Miss Anderson?'

Again Max felt that apprehensive chill in his stomach. For all the casualness in the question, something warned him that behind those flat, grey eyes a keen brain was at work, like some dynamo, seizing upon anything that was the slightest suspicious, and building up his evidence bit by bit. He said:

'When the business about her uncle's coat cropped up, Miss Anderson had gone to 'phone for the doctor. I didn't see her to talk to until this morning.'

'That's right,' Parry said. 'After they'd left me.'

'So only the four of us here know anything about all this? The possibility it might be foul play, I mean.'

'Plus whoever pushed him — if he was pushed,' Dan remarked.

'Quite.' Morris stared a trifle moodily at the gleaming surface of the table for a few moments. Then he stood up and glanced at the clock on the wall. 'This has all the earmarks of a job for Divisional H.Q.,' he said. 'I'll 'phone Caernarvon.'

'And see what the superintendent has to say?' Parry asked.

The other nodded. 'He'll be on to the Vernon idea fast enough. And he'll want to dig into Jones' death sure enough.'

'Which means Caernarvon C.I.D. will take over?' Again Parry put the question, and Dan glanced at Max.

'Criminal Investigation Department stuff?' he said.

Morris eyed him. 'You're both staying in the district for the next few days, you say?' And in answer to Dan's emphatically affirmative nod: 'In case you might like to talk to Caernarvon.'

'Or in case they might like to talk to us,' Max said.

'They'll find us at the Crooked Inn,' Dan said. 'Until after the funeral anyway. We're going back there after lunch.'

Sergeant Morris's tone was heavy. 'I know I can count on you to keep this under your hats still. Aside from avoiding scaring off Vernon — if he *is* in the vicinity — Caernarvon will want to make their inquiries very discreetly, if you follow me.'

'I think we get the general idea,' Max said.

The other paused then went on. 'But the atmosphere at the pub must be a bit morbid? You don't want to rush back to Mynydd Llanberis — why not take advantage of the nice day?' He indicated the blue sky framed by the windows, with only a few crisp, white clouds in the distance. 'Make a trip up Snowdon.'

'That's a notion,' Dan turned to Max. 'Why don't we do that?'

Max agreed. It seemed a good idea to get their lungs full of fresh air and try and take their minds off the grim happenings of the past few hours.

'Day like this,' Parry the Police was saying, 'visibility will be tip-top — you'll be able to see as far as the Irish Sea, and that's a fact.'

'But I don't want to see the Irish Sea,' Dan objected. 'I'm a bad sailor.'

There was a dutiful laugh from Parry

166

and they were all standing up now, Dan and Max preparing to take their departure.

'We'll show our faces at the Criccieth Arms,' Max told Dan, who asked:

'Wonder if we dare ask 'em for lunch?'

Max thought they might.

Some time later the two of them were drinking their coffee in the restaurant of the Criccieth Arms, which overlooked the mountain railway-station. From their table by the window they could see the miniature engine and carriages drawn up alongside the platform, awaiting the time of the next ascent. Dan had been extolling the especial qualities possessed by the people of North Wales.

'All nice people in this part of the world. Simple and kind. Don't let themselves be kidded by our atomic age superficialities, but hold fast to the eternal verities.' To Max's slightly absent murmur of agreement, he went on. 'Take Sergeant Morris. Could you meet a more human, genial copper if you tried?'

'I haven't tried to meet many. I wouldn't say he was so simple.'

'Oh, nothing of the comedy rustic flatfoot about him.'

'I found his solicitude for our welfare quite touching,' Max said, a faintly sardonic smile at the corners of his mouth. 'Suggesting we enjoy the view from Snowdon. Instead of brooding in the depressing atmosphere of the Crooked Inn.'

The other caught the mocking note in his voice, and said sharply: 'Nothing wrong with that.'

Max gave a slight shrug. 'Could be,' he said, 'he really wanted to make sure we'd be clear of the place for an hour or two.'

Dan's spoon was poised over his coffee-cup. 'Why should he?'

'I daresay he might have his reasons.'

'But, my dear Max,' Dan said, 'surely he can't think we're a couple of crooks?'

'I was merely wondering.'

'You're on the wrong track, really you are.' Then he said: 'All right for the play, of course . . . ' He shook his head and grinned. 'Though I'm not altogether sure it's good even for that.'

They quitted the hotel and presently found themselves in the train, chugging up the mountain. The carriages were open at the sides and on either side of them Caernarvonshire was spread out. Greens and browns and a sparkle of water where the sun caught at the surface of a lake. Ahead of them the single track snaked up the mountain-side, with on their left the great chasm of Llanberis Pass. Now and again as the little train curved and twisted on its ascent they caught glimpses of the road far below, toy-like cars speeding along it and an ant-like figure here and there.

The air was magnificent, they were filled with a feeling of extraordinary exhilaration. Higher and higher the train puffed, more and more of the countryside stretched away on either side of them. Moors, dotted with farms and the white specks of sheep, and woods and the Snowdon Range: its mountains curving and flowing like huge billows, in masses of green and brown, blending into the misty blue of the horizon.

'We certainly couldn't have picked a

better day for it,' Dan extended an arm towards the panorama on their left.

'This place we're coming to? Is this Half-way House, as they call it?'

They were approaching a wooden shack on the right of the track, down the slope where the footpath ran. It was obviously a café.

'That's it — ' Dan began, and then broke off with an exclamation. 'Do you see what I see?'

'I rather fancy I do.'

'The woman outside the place — it's Miss Kimber.'

'It's her all right.'

They stared at the figure which was now past the café and heading forward determinedly along the rough track. There was no doubt it was Miss Kimber. Obviously she had caught the bus to Llanberis with the object of making the ascent of Snowdon on foot.

'She's more athletic than you might think,' Dan said, as she strode vigorously on. She did not glance at the train, or they might have waved at her.

'What about hopping off at the next

stop?' Dan asked. 'And walking down to meet her?'

'With what idea?'

'Just a sort of hunch I had, or something. I'd like to see her surprised look at bumping into us out of the blue.' Dan shrugged. 'But don't let me interrupt your trip. I can hop off and you can go on up, and we'll meet up later.'

Max waved the suggestion aside. 'I'm as much intrigued as you arc by the deceptive Miss Kimber.' He glanced at the figure striding along the path below.

'Deceptive is right.'

'We'll hop off at the next station.'

Dan nodded. 'Clogwyn Coch it's called,' he said.

The station was no more than a hut with a levelled-out space for passengers to ascend or descend. The train puffing and chugging fussily, drew to a stop. Max and Dan got off the train and watched it for a few moments as it pursued its course up the mountain-side. It seemed like some caterpillar eating its way round the curve of Snowdon, its nose irrevocably fixed towards the summit.

A signpost at the side of the track told them they were over two thousand feet above sea-level. They stood surveying the marvellous vista below them. The sky was a brilliant blue, the sun beat down warm and bright. They took in deep gulps of glorious air.

'We can make the trip all the way to the top another time,' Dan was saying. 'I don't feel we should miss this chance of meeting Miss Kimber this way. Isn't that a wonderful view of Llanberis Pass?' He pointed at the huge gap in the mountain below them.

Llanberis itself was hidden, but they could see the waters of Lake Padarn, which ran out of the village. 'What's that small lake on the left?' Max asked. It was a tiny pool of water bright against the green and brown gorse surrounding it. It glittered bright blue, a Mediterranean blue, beneath the sky, like some turquoise in a magical setting.

'That must be what they call Lyn Ffynon Gwas.' Pointing out the direction from which they had come, Dan went on:

'That would be just about where Mynydd Llanberis lies.'

'Further to your left, Mynydd Llanberis,' a cracked voice said behind them and they turned to encounter a very old man. They had not noticed him when they had left the train. He looked as if he might have been a shepherd. His leathery skin was a mass of wrinkles and folds, and a pair of bright black eyes peered at them from under an old cap. He carried a crooked stick upon which he leaned heavily as he stood there.

Dan thanked him for his information.

'Lies almost due north from here, Mynydd Llanberis does,' the old chap said. He waved his stick. 'See the Crooked Mountain over there?'

They saw a peak to their left, which rose on the other side of Llanberis Pass, its sides green and patched with gorse, and then becoming a spire of jagged rock. It twisted and curved grotesquely, so that its name seemed an ideal one for it.

'The Crooked Mountain, eh?' Dan echoed.

'Like a corkscrew,' Max said.

173

'Then the inn must be just the other side of it,' Dan said.

'Used to be a copper-mine there,' the old man was croaking again. 'Years ago. Not working now,' he added. 'Not since the accident and a miner was killed.'

'We've heard about that,' Dan said.

'Some say it's haunted. No one ever goes near it, anyhow. Too scared, people are.' And the old man stared at the strangely shaped peak, screwing up his eyes in their folds of wrinkles and weather-beaten flesh. Dan winked at Max.

'We'd better be moving,' he said. 'If we aren't careful our Miss Kimber will have passed us and reached the top of Snowdon.' They began to move off, turning back to their informant with a word of thanks. The old man assured them they were welcome and waved his stick to them.

As they moved down the side of the railway track nearest the footpath along which Miss Kimber must presently be expected, Max said: 'A thought for the play, by the way. I was wondering if we could use a character like Miss Kimber who turns out to be a man disguised. And is, of course, the head crook.'

'Dressed up as a man?' Dan regarded him dubiously. 'Bit difficult to swallow, don't you think?'

'That's what worries *me*. Only there was a real-life case — '

He broke off and stared out across towards the Crooked Mountain. He stood stock-still, a hand on Dan's arm.

'What have you seen?' Dan said.

'Someone on the mountain.'

Something in the other's tones caused Dan to glance at him sharply. 'I thought the old boy just said nobody ever goes there? Too scared.'

'It's a woman,' Max said slowly, still staring across at the mountain. '*She's* not scared — '

'A woman?' Dan followed his fixed gaze. 'Don't tell me our athletic Miss Kimber's taken a flying leap?'

'It isn't her,' Max said. 'It's Wynne Anderson.'

8

The grandfather's-clock at the foot of the staircase struck three-thirty as old Price paused in the door of the Crooked Inn and sneezed. He went in and Roberts materialised from the shadows to greet him.

'There you are. On the dot.'

The old man peered at him, his eyes dazzled by the sunlight and requiring a minute or two in which to get used to the shadowy lounge. 'Oh, it's you, Mr. Roberts.'

'Miss Anderson will appreciate you being so punctual.'

'I didn't want to keep her waiting,' Price said politely. 'She is expecting me?'

'She's expecting you, never fear.'

'You told her it was something important I wanted to see her about?'

Roberts took the cigarette from the corner of his mouth and exhaled slowly. Beneath his unwinking gaze the old man shifted from one foot to the other. There was something about Roberts' attitude which filled him with a certain uneasiness. He thought he detected a smirk of what might be secret triumph on those dark, sharp features.

'As I promised you I would,' the other was telling him, suavely. 'Without saying what it was.'

Old Price relaxed somewhat. He gave Roberts a grateful nod. 'Very kind of you.'

'It's my duty to do all I can to help get this business cleared up.' Roberts went on, after a moment's hesitation: 'The only thing is, Miss Anderson — er — isn't here.'

'But you said — '

'I know what I said, and she still wants to see you.'

Price peered at him from under his bristling eyebrows, and pushing his cap back, scratched his head. 'You mean,' he said slowly, 'Miss Anderson isn't in, and I'm to wait till she gets back?'

'Er — no . . . ' Roberts eyed him cautiously, as if he was weighing every word. 'The idea,' he said, 'is for you to meet her.'

Price didn't catch what he said. 'Eh?'

'You're to meet her,' Roberts raised his voice. 'Somewhere else.'

'Meet her somewhere else? Where?'

'You see, with the guests coming in for tea, it wouldn't have been easy for you to talk to her. Not quietly.'

'I suppose it might have been a bit awkward.' But the old man's expression was still puzzled.

'And we don't want to risk anyone overhearing you.'

That was true enough, Price told himself. He didn't want Parry the Police, for instance, to know he had been out at that late hour last night, only put suspicions in his mind, Parry being the nasty, creeping, sneaking sort he was. He heard Roberts saying:

'So Miss Anderson said will you meet her where the footpath starts up to Crooked Mountain?'

Price stared at him, his mouth open. 'But that path,' he found his voice, 'is the one leading to — to — '

'Well?'

'To the old copper-mine.'

'That's it,' Roberts said briskly. 'There'll be nobody about and you can talk without fear of interruption.'

Price continued to eye him without any degree of enthusiasm. 'I should think there will be nobody about,' he grumbled. 'You know as well as I do, no one dare go near the place, being that scared.'

'Night-time, I know,' Roberts said airily, 'it *is* — well — supposed to be haunted.'

'I've heard you say yourself nothing on God's earth would tempt you there.'

'I know, I know. But I don't suppose it's a bit frightening in daylight.'

But the other still remained unimpressed. 'Why did you have to pick on that eerie place?'

'I didn't pick on it. It was Miss Anderson. Not living in these parts and not believing in local superstitions and her being young and so on — ' He broke off and shrugged. 'It's only where the path begins,' he pointed out. 'It isn't at the old mine itself.'

'I should hope it isn't,' Price gave a shudder. He tugged his cap over the bridge of his nose indecisively. Then he seemed to make up his mind. 'All right . . . Suppose I'd best get along.'

The other regarded the tip of his cigarette thoughtfully. Then replacing it in the corner of his mouth he said, elaborately casual: 'You'd better if you want her to hear your story of what you saw last night.'

'Yes, I've got to tell her all about that.'

'I've plenty to do,' Roberts said with a change of tone, as he eyed the old man, who still stood there, his attitude undecided. 'The teas to fix for when they start coming in.'

Price gave a start as if he had been awoken from a reverie, then started to shuffle to the door. 'I still can't see why Miss Anderson had to choose that spot,' he wheezed over his shoulder. 'But there it is.' He turned at the door. 'See you later, Mr. Roberts.'

As the old man went out Roberts moved after him with that cat-like tread to the doorway. Standing back in the shadow he watched Price shambling off down the road. There was a smile on his thin lips, then he turned and went along to the kitchen.

Price came to the stile and clambered over it, grumbling to himself at the rheumatic twinges the effort cost him. The Crooked Inn lay behind him, hidden by a wooded hill, and to his right scrubby moorland and low slopes formed the base of the Crooked Mountain. Left, fields extended until they merged into moorland that too rose into the rocky foothills of Snowdon. Ahead of him ran the narrow footpath that angled behind a rocky mound before it inclined upwards towards the beginning of the copper-mine workings.

He could see no signs of Miss Anderson as he steadied himself and began to move along the path. The place was lonely and possessed a curiously desolate atmosphere, although the sun still shone in the cloudless sky. He glanced about him. There was no one to be seen. Not even a shepherd, or a dog. Only distant blobs of white on the mountain-side that were sheep. He could not repress a shudder. He turned and scowled at the Crooked Mountain, the ugly way it spiralled upwards, all twisted and tortured-looking, it was.

Like some strange animal in its death agonies, it seemed to Price. He could glimpse that part of the mountain where he knew the old copper-mine ran into the earth, burrowing upwards to emerge somewhere on the other side. He was approaching the outcrop of rock that pushed its way out of the ground and behind which the path disappeared. Still no sign of Miss Anderson. He had expected any moment she would make her appearance. He wondered where she could be. Unless she was round the other side of the rock? Yet he would have thought she would have kept a look-out for him. Or perhaps she had strolled further along the path?

He didn't think she could have become impatient and given him up, he had come along as soon as he could. He rounded the rock and paused. No one there. He scratched his head in dismay and puzzlement. Overhead the bough of a tree which overhung the path creaked slightly.

Old Price stood there hesitantly and was about to turn on his heel, when there was a sudden movement from behind the tree-trunk.

'Hello, Mr. Price.'

There was a glint of spectacles and then something in the approaching figure's expression caused Price to gasp, the words he wanted to speak sticking in his throat. He tried to run, but sheer terror robbed his old limbs of what little strength they possessed so that he could not move.

9

There was no mistaking the slim figure, even at that distance. The red-gold hair glinted in the sunlight as she began to move towards where a narrow path began. In the clear air of the bright day she stood out against the green of the mountain-side, sharply defined.

'Wonder what she's doing there?' Dan asked after a few moments.

'Just taking a stroll,' Max's tone was light.

Dan shot a look at him. Then his gaze returned to the girl. 'I hope she's safe.'

'Safe?' Max eyed him. 'Safe from what?'

'The mountain being haunted, and all that,' Dan said. 'I mean, it might be dangerous.'

'It looks remarkably unhaunted from where we're standing. Just a nice, friendly mountain same as the rest.'

'All the same, that old boy spoke as if

there was something odd about it. The place has obviously got a reputation with the locals.'

'Local superstitions have a way of being built up out of nothing,' Max said.

Dan nodded agreement. They watched Wynne Anderson gain the path which vanished behind a shoulder jutting out from the mountain. Now she herself, following the path, disappeared.

'All the same,' Dan said after a moment, 'I don't like the idea of her wandering around like that. I mean, if it was Vernon who killed her uncle — '

'There's no proof of that,' Max put in.

'No proof, I know,' the other admitted, 'but it shapes up that way. Whoever it was they might be planning to get her out of the way next.'

Max regarded him narrowly. 'I don't quite see why *she* should be in any danger.'

The girl had not reappeared. Max was frowning a little to himself, Dan noted. He said: 'Anyway I admit there's not much we can do about it from here. She's gone. I suggest we hurry on down to

Half-way House and meet up with Miss Kimber.'

They crossed the railway track and made their way down the bank to the pathway below. The grass was slippery and they were forced to half-run and half-slide past rocks and marshy patches which rose up before them. A bird winged upwards suddenly from beneath their feet and soared high into the air, singing warningly as it did so. Dan was chuckling involuntarily as he and Max plunged on, until they reached the path and were able to proceed down it at a more leisurely, less hazardous pace.

The wooden structure that was the café, outside which they had spotted Miss Kimber, came into sight — and they had not yet encountered the schoolmistress. Dan turned a perplexed look on Max. 'We could hardly have missed her on the way down.'

Max shook his head. 'And there hasn't been another train she could have hopped into.'

'Which leaves only one explanation. She must have turned back after we'd seen her.' Dan glanced at his watch. It was approaching half-past three. 'Maybe she was thinking of her tea waiting for her at the Crooked Inn.'

'Could be.'

'Which is an idea, come to think,' Dan said. 'I could use a nice cup of tea myself. This mountain climbing's thirsty work.'

'I'd hardly describe sitting in a train and walking half a mile downhill as mountain climbing,' he said.

'You're just splitting hairs.' They both turned at the sound of a train behind them. It was bound for Llanberis — and with a yell and wildly waving his arms at it, Dan dashed up the slope. 'We'll hop aboard this,' he shouted over his shoulder. 'If we can pick up a bus for Mynydd Llanberis we'll arrive in time to join Miss Kimber for tea.'

Max followed him and they reached the stopping-place in time to board the train. Max was silent as they chugged and puffed fussily down, joining only half-heartedly in Dan's exuberant admiration for the vista that flowed past them. Presently they were rattling across the bridge over the Ceunant Mawr. The awe-inspiring waterfall, gushing from a huge cleft, tumbled sixty feet below into a boiling cauldron of creamy foam before it sped on its way to Lake Padarn. The wind blew a curtain of fine spray in the train's path. Caught by the sunlight, the mist sparkled and caused a rainbow of colours before Max's eyes. But he could see only the slim, lonely figure on the mountain-side.

They hurried out of Llanberis Station just in time to catch a bus to Mynydd Llanberis.

There was no one in the lounge as they went into the inn. Round the fireplace, in which logs had been placed in readiness for the chill of the evening, tables were laid for tea. But either Miss Kimber hadn't arrived, or, which seemed unlikely, she had somehow returned before them, had her tea and gone. Their arrival brought Roberts into the lounge.

'Miss Anderson has told me you'll both be staying on for a day or two longer.'

'Which news I'm sure,' Max said, 'made you more than happy.'

'Afraid, sir, it isn't a very happy house, just at the moment.'

'We your only clients this afternoon?'

'Miss Kimber should be here any minute. She always is in for meals. Except lunch today,' with a slight frown. 'She 'phoned to say she would be going over to Llanberis.'

''Phoned? Where from?'

The other looked at him as if he was about to inquire what business it was of his where Miss Kimber 'phoned from. Instead he said: 'From a call-box down the road. Before she caught the bus to Llanberis, I suppose.'

Dan nodded. 'Perhaps she's staying there for tea as well?'

'She never mentioned that.'

'How about Mr. Darrell?'

'Never back before dinner, Mr. Darrell isn't. Takes sandwiches when he goes off after breakfast.'

'Too engrossed waiting for the fish to bite to worry overmuch about his own food, eh?' Dan said.

Roberts muttered something about how Mr. Darrell was a very keen fisherman and then made to move off to get their tea. He was halted by Max inquiring after Wynne.

'Miss Anderson's managing all right, sir. They've — er — taken Mr. Jones away,' he added in an appropriately funereal tone.

'Who's they?' Dan asked.

'From Bangor, I think. Parry the Police was here. Routine, he said it was. Police always have to examine the body when it's sudden death.'

'Oh, yes,' Dan said with well-simulated casualness, and restraining a knowing glance at Max. 'I suppose they do have to wrap up the business with red tape.'

'Where is Miss Anderson?' Max asked.

'Gone up to her room, sir. Hasn't long come in from a breath of fresh air.' At this piece of information Dan found it impossible not to throw Max a look, which the latter, however, did not return. Roberts had asked: 'Do you want to see Miss Anderson, sir?'

'Perhaps a little later,' Max said.

Roberts nodded and hurried off, Max staring after him for a moment before turning to Dan.

'So she's not long back from a breath of fresh air, eh?' he said thoughtfully.

'That's what he said. You'd have thought she could have found all the fresh air she needed, without having to climb half-way up a mountain for it.'

'She may have been feeling so upset she didn't realise where she was walking.' But Dan didn't think Max spoke with a great deal of conviction.

'You going to ask her?'

Max eyed him for a moment, without replying. He took out his pipe, tapped the bowl and saw it was empty, made as if to reach for his tobacco-pouch, then remembering tea was on its way returned the pipe to his pocket. 'I don't know,' he said slowly. 'The fact that she was there needn't mean anything one way or another. I don't suppose there's any law against wandering round the Crooked Mountain.'

'It just seems a little odd, somehow.' Dan threw himself into a chair beside one of the tables laid for tea. 'Anyhow, I'd watch out, if I were you.'

Max regarded him with a faintly

amused look. 'Watch out?'

'I was thinking of Sergeant Morris's warning about not letting anyone suspect anything.'

Dan, Max realised, was visualising the possibility of the girl's allure causing him to talk too much. He decided to ignore the implication, however, and at that moment Roberts appeared with the tea. As he put down the tray, well-laden with bread-and-butter, Welsh honey and a selection of cakes, he said conversationally:

'I expect you'll both be hungry, after your trip to — er — wherever it was.'

'We'll do our best to do justice to what looks like a pretty substantial tea, Roberts,' Dan said, giving Max a wink across the dark head bent momentarily over the tea-table.

But Roberts, attempting as seemed obvious enough, to elicit information concerning the object of their excursion, was nothing if not persistent. 'Most exceptional scenery round these parts,' he said. 'You were lucky with the weather, too.'

'Couldn't have picked a better day if we'd ordered it,' Dan agreed enthusiastically. Roberts turned to him, the innocence of his expression sitting uncomfortably on his saturnine features.

'Though, of course,' he said, 'I don't know what particular part of the scenery you were most interested in.'

'It was all superb,' Dan afforded himself a broad grin at the other's transparent and continued efforts to find out where their trip had taken them. 'Superb,' he repeated, 'and that's a fact.' He turned to Max. 'Shall I be mum?' he queried.

'I see you've picked up a local phrase, sir,' Roberts was observing.

Dan looked at him sharply. 'Have I?' he asked.

'Parry the Police's favourite expression is: 'That's a fact.''

Dan repressed a start. So that was what lay behind the curious note in the other's voice. 'Parry — ?' he began, slightly flustered, then conscious of Max's eye on him, recovered himself and asked more coolly: 'Is it really?'

'Always using it, he is.' A thin smile curved Roberts' mouth, a bright gleam flashed in his eye. 'Did you walk, sir? To where you went, I mean. Or were you able to get a bus?'

'Talking of which,' Dan said, ignoring this last query, 'I hope Miss Kimber hasn't missed her bus.'

Roberts seemed to realise he was getting nowhere fast. He gave up. 'I can't think she has,' he said, 'or I'm sure she would have 'phoned.'

'Prim and punctilious type, Miss Kimber, isn't she?' Dan spread some Welsh honey liberally on some home-baked bread-and-butter.

'Very.'

'Stayed here before?' Max asked.

'Not as far as I know, sir.'

'How long have you been here, Roberts?' Dan said, giving the other a searching look.

'Me, sir? Getting on for eighteen months.'

'I suppose you'll have to find a job elsewhere?' Dan asked.

Roberts met his gaze with a bland

expression. 'That will be for Miss Anderson to decide, sir.' He turned away abruptly with an: 'If you'll excuse me — there's nothing else you require at the moment?'

'Oh, don't let us think we're driving you away,' Dan grinned at him. The other paused, his hands down at his side, his head thrust forward slightly. If he was about to make any retort, he changed his mind and with that feline movement hurried away.

Dan finished consuming his bread-and-honey. Then in a carefully lowered voice, he said to Max: 'Soon pushed off when *we* started asking him the questions.'

Max nodded over his cup of tea.

'Wonder how much he *does* know about the goings-on here?' Dan mused. 'More than he'll admit, I shouldn't wonder.' He took another slice of bread-and-butter. 'I bet Parry the Police is fairly wallowing in all this.'

'Must make a change from bikes with no lights and poachers like old Price to cope with.'

'A murder must be a day to chalk up in the life of a village cop.'

'*Suspected* murder,' Max reminded him.

'Who'd have thought,' he said, 'when we got into the car at Bangor Station last night, we'd be driven head first into a plot like this.'

'We certainly owe Price a vote of thanks for landing us at the wrong pub.'

'Definitely. He won't think we owe him a cut out of our royalties?'

'I'm sure a ticket for the first night will do,' Max said.

Dan's face grew serious and he leaned across the table. 'And for us the play *is* more important than all these odd happenings around us — '

'I've managed to scribble down a few notes,' Max said, pouring himself another cup of tea.

'Me, too. And, of course, all this drama and mystery we've butted into *is* terrific material.'

'What you're getting at,' Max leaned back, reaching for his pipe, and tobacco-pouch, 'is we're going to be saddled with a headache licking the characters and incidents that have happened here into the shape we can use.'

'Exactly.'

Max tamped the tobacco down into the bowl of his pipe and thoughtfully struck a match. 'And for all we know things haven't *stopped* happening.'

Dan gave him a sudden look. 'Don't say that,' he said in mock protest. 'We've got all the material we want, surely. We can carry on very nicely now and finish off the plot our way.'

'Depends if the Crooked Inn will oblige,' Max said through a cloud of tobacco-smoke.

Dan eyed him for a moment. 'We just sit tight in our ringside seats and see it through.'

'I fancy that's what Sergeant Morris and Co. would prefer us to do.'

Dan drained his cup of tea and pushed himself back in his chair thoughtfully. 'I'd forgotten them.'

'They're as good a reason as any for staying to see what happens next.' Max looked up suddenly as a figure appeared at the top of the stairs.

Dan leaned forward and said under his breath: 'And here comes another reason for you to stick around.'

10

'I thought I'd see if you were being looked after properly,' Wynne Anderson said. With a wan smile she refused the cigarette Dan offered her. Dan lit his own cigarette.

'We've just made beasts of ourselves over a colossal tea.'

'Good,' she hesitated for a moment. Then she said to Max: 'Did you get on all right at Llanberis?'

'Fine, thanks.'

'The hotel people couldn't have been pleasanter about our change of plan,' Dan said.

'I'm glad to see you're looking better,' Max said.

'I've been out for some fresh air.'

'Roberts told us.'

'The mountain air's marvellously reviving,' Dan said. They both watched her face. She gave no sign of having understood the implication in the last remark. She turned away a little. Max felt a twinge of remorse at this somewhat crude attempt to trap her. As if Dan had in fact spoken in all innocence he said:

'We took a trip half-way up Snowdon.'

'Did you?' She turned back to them. 'That's wonderfully exhilarating, isn't it?' They both agreed it was an experience worth enjoying and she went on: 'Miss Kimber hasn't returned yet. She was going over to Llanberis, she told Roberts.'

Dan mentioned that Roberts had appeared quite perturbed about the schoolteacher. There was a silence. Dan looked at Max. He seemed absorbed in the examination of his pipe bowl. Dan glanced at the girl who was staring abstractedly towards the window. He muttered something about going to see if Miss Kimber could be seen and moved towards the door. He stood there for a few moments watching but there was no sign of the school-mistress, and he turned back into the room.

The girl was saying to Max: 'I hope all — all this hasn't upset your plans for working?'

Max shook his head and Dan said: 'Which reminds me, I must toddle upstairs and look as if I'm doing some work.' To the girl: 'If you'll excuse me.'

She inclined her head. 'You must forgive me,' Dan said, 'if I say that no matter what goes on around me, it never stops me from writing. Come hell or high water, the play's the thing.' He went quickly upstairs.

Max turned to the girl.

'If you want to work, too — ' she began, but he interrupted her.

'I'd rather stay and talk to you.'

'I thought Mr. Evans,' she said, 'went off rather — well — hurriedly. As if you ought to follow him, and not waste time here with me.'

'I suppose,' Max replied slowly, 'he realises that when you come on the scene my interests are no longer wrapped up in the play exclusively.'

'Oh, dear . . . What do I say now?'

'I must admit,' he said, 'I've rather run out of dialogue myself.'

'Fine thing for a playwright to confess.'

'This isn't a play we're writing.'

'We're writing?'

'I hope it's going to be a collaboration.'

'I thought you said you'd run out of dialogue?' she mocked him. There was an elaborately discreet cough behind them and Roberts came into the room.

He busied himself clearing the table and then stood, the laden tray in his hands. 'I'll give Miss Kimber a few more minutes, Miss Anderson.' In answer to her nod he went out.

Max looked after him for a moment, then turned to the girl. 'Talking of the missing Miss Kimber,' he said.

'Were we?'

'Dan and I saw her this afternoon. Half-way up Snowdon. We were in the train, but she was fairly charging up the mountain-path. We got off at the next stop,' he went on. 'With the idea of walking down to meet her.'

He paused and looked at her. She returned his gaze steadily and appeared to be waiting for him to continue. He didn't say anything, however. Took his pipe out of his mouth, saw it was cold and lit another match.

'I expect she was surprised to see you,' she said at last.

'She didn't,' he said over the flame of his match. Then he asked her abruptly: 'You know Snowdon, don't you?' She said she'd made the trip a couple of times, though not walking. 'Then,' he said, 'I don't have to tell you how you can see for miles around,' and she said she was prepared to admit the views were perfectly lovely and he continued. 'Some old chap told us the name of a rather pretty lake,' and she said, her eyes wide behind her spectacles, as if she was wondering where all this was leading to, that she knew the name of the lake he meant, only she couldn't remember it now, and he said: 'Then . . . he pointed out the Crooked Mountain.'

Her head was a little on one side, so that a thick lock of her hair fell forward and made a bronze shadow on one side of her face and he could feel his heart beating a little too fast.

'Didn't you know you could see it from Snowdon?' And waited for her reply.

'I'd forgotten.'

'The old chap explained how this inn was the other side of it.'

'It would be.'

'He was saying how they used to work a copper-mine there.' Max could see her hands, they were small, but capable-looking hands, twisting in each other nervously. 'Until a miner was killed in an accident.'

Her hands dropped to her sides. Her voice took on a slight edginess. 'I've heard Roberts talk about it. It was a long time ago.'

'One of his favourite topics of conversation, I gather.'

She was starting to turn away again, so that he caught the line of her profile, soft in the subdued light of the lounge. He noted the tenseness at the corner of her mouth and his heart constricted, and he found it difficult to continue to feel suspicious. But why wouldn't she admit she had been out there on the Crooked Mountain? Why did she try to sheer off the subject?

'He is inclined to dwell on it,' she was saying now. 'When he gets talking.'

'This old boy went on about how the locals are too scared to go near the mountain. Supposed to be haunted.'

She swung back to him. Her eyes bright and staring full at him. 'I'd like a cigarette.' He started to shake his head, to explain he didn't have any cigarettes on him, but she had got a case from her handbag. She took a cigarette and her hand was firm as she held it while he lit it for her.

'There is some silly gossip about the mountain,' she said.

'You don't believe in that sort of thing?'

She shook her head, smiling at him. A mocking smile? He didn't know. He said:

'It wouldn't scare *you* off . . . if you had reason to go there?'

She considered the question for a moment. 'I might feel a bit nervous,' she admitted slowly. 'Perhaps. But,' she said, 'if the reason was good enough, I suppose I'd go.'

'Was the reason good enough this afternoon?'

Her expression didn't alter. Had she, he wondered now, been steeling herself to answer him without allowing him to see that she was affected unduly? She spoke in a low voice.

'I don't quite see what concern it is of yours.'

He was about to take her hand understandingly. Instead he stood quite still. 'I am concerned about you. You know that. When I saw you — '

'How did you, by the way?' Her face was raised to him with interest.

'Pure chance. I happened to be looking at the scenery from Half-way House.'

She gave a frankly rueful laugh. 'You would have to do that, wouldn't you?'

'Look,' he said. 'Wynne . . . I know it's no business of mine. But when I saw you there, it seemed rather — well — odd. I mean it is a sinister spot, and under the circumstances — '

'It was *because* of the circumstances,' she cut in. 'Because of Uncle's death, that I went.' He eyed her curiously and she continued. 'I've found out something,' she said. 'About him. Something — '

She broke off as he made a sudden movement, twisting round on his heel.

'Thought I heard a step,' he nodded

towards the passage to the kitchen. 'Out there.'

As he spoke Roberts appeared. 'No sign of Miss Kimber,' he said to the girl. 'I might as well clear.'

'Very well, Roberts. I'm sure Miss Kimber won't be back for tea, now.'

Max glanced at her and then at Roberts. She interpreted his look and nodded. She spoke to him in a carefully casual tone. 'I'm going to the office, Mr. Mitchell. Would you care to come with me? I can show you the — er — photographs I was talking about.'

'I'd like to see them.'

He followed after her, pausing to turn and look at Roberts. But the man was bent busily over the table, removing the tea-things on to a tray. Wynne closed the office door, and he stood leaning against it, watching her.

'I was wondering what Roberts must be wondering about us,' she said. 'Did I seem very brazen?'

'So long as he doesn't guess what you are going to tell me,' he said. 'About your uncle.'

'I don't know that I ought to worry you with my troubles.'

He moved towards her. 'That's why I wanted to stay on here. To help you.'

Her eyes were smoky and warm. She touched his coat and his hand closed over hers. Gently, yet firmly. 'You're very sweet . . . Max. I can't believe we hadn't met before last night.'

'Was it only last night? So it was. What were you going to tell me, before Roberts barged in?'

She hesitated, then said, and her voice sank much lower: 'It's this feeling I have. That there was something strange about Uncle's death.'

There was a short pause. He searched her face. She met his gaze steadily. 'In what way?' He kept his voice down.

'I *don't* believe in feminine intuition, but — '

'As intuitions go, it's as good as any other kind,' he encouraged her.

'But something seems to keep telling me it — it, well, it wasn't an accident.'

'But you've no real reason for thinking this?'

She shook her head helplessly. 'If I had, I suppose I'd have gone to Parry.'

An arrow of late afternoon sunlight speeding through the window, shot through her marvellous hair. She ran her tongue along her lower lip, and it glistened in the sunlight. He resisted an almost overpowering impulse to take her in his arms. She was saying:

'It's just a silly nagging at the back of my mind.'

'Nothing about your uncle,' Max asked her, 'for instance, suggested he might have an enemy?'

She hesitated, a shadow in her eyes. 'There again, only an increasing sense there was something wrong.'

'How long had you had this hunch about him?'

The girl thought for a moment before she answered. 'The last eighteen months. Before then,' she told him, 'he was always such fun. But lately it was as if there was something on his mind. He *said* it was the worry of running this place, but it was more than that.'

Max was staring at her. He said half to

himself: 'Eighteen months . . . ' Then to her: 'About the time Roberts came here?'

'Roberts?' A frown crossed her face. 'What could he have to do with it?'

'Just a thought, that's all.'

'I know he's sour-faced and grouchy,' she said defensively, 'but he works well. I'm sure he couldn't have any influence over Uncle.'

He had the impression she was not entirely convincing herself. All the same he decided to agree with her. 'What did you find out from your uncle that sent you to the Crooked Mountain?'

As if to prove to him he was mistaken about Roberts, she moved swiftly to the door and pulled it open. There was no one there. She stood gazing into the lounge and then turned back and closed the door again. With an I-told-you-so smile, she crossed to the desk underneath the window and pulled out a drawer. He watched her as she rummaged under what seemed to be a miscellany of letters, bills and odds and ends. She drew out a folded piece of paper and handed it to him. He took it from her and unfolded it.

It was stained and its edges tattered. It bore a crudely drawn plan headed: 'The Crooked Mountain Copper-Mine.'

'I came across it behind those books a day or two ago. I meant to ask Uncle about it.' She pointed over his shoulder to some fresher-looking markings. 'There's a shaft at the top of the mine that leads to a path on to the mountain.' He looked up at her questioningly. 'That's where you saw me this afternoon.'

That explained it, he told himself. What she had told him certainly lifted any hint of suspicion there might have been against her. The tiny warning bell he had fancied he had heard ringing at the back of his mind was silenced.

'I wanted to find out what this bit of paper was all in aid of,' she was saying. 'I remembered how Uncle was so late back last night, and I suddenly wondered if it was because he'd been there,' she indicated the plan Max was still holding, 'and had been forced to shelter there during the storm.'

'What made you think of the copper-mine?'

'I also remembered his coat being rather muddy when he came in, as if he'd been scrambling along the wet ground.'

'Quite the girl detective.' But she didn't smile back at him. 'So you climbed the shaft,' he continued, 'found the path, and it led to — ?'

'I don't know. I — I turned back.'

He could not keep the surprise out of his face and the tone of his voice. 'After having got so far?'

'It became a narrow ledge,' she said with a slight shudder of recollection. 'A sheer drop, round a jutting-out rock.'

'Sounds interesting.'

'That's why I wanted to see round the other side,' she said. 'But I haven't a good head for heights.'

He nodded thoughtfully. The question posed by her account of her visit to the mountain-side was decidedly intriguing. He could imagine Dan's reaction to all he would have to tell him: the tattered old plan of the disused copper-mine, the girl's story of the dangerously narrow path . . . Max smiled to himself as he imagined Dan's eyes gleam at the dramatic possibilities unfolded. He directed his attention back to Wynne Anderson.

'You think that on the other side of the rock might lie the answer to the mystery about your uncle?'

'I don't know,' she answered. 'But . . . ' Her voice trailed away.

He returned his attention to the piece of paper he was holding. He spread it out on the desk. 'Doesn't it show anything here?'

She was beside him examining the plan. 'I'm afraid it's no help,' she said.

He ran his forefinger over the drawing. There was the top of the shaft marked in the newer ink. Here was the path running from the exit from the shaft — the path Wynne had followed that afternoon, until she had been unable to proceed further. After that nothing was indicated, merely a few straggling dots which tailed off. It occurred to Max that whoever had made the additions to the old chart had not wanted to run the risk of putting what lay beyond the rock down on paper. He folded up the plan and gave it back to the girl. She took it and pushed it back under

213

the oddments in the drawer and closed it again.

'Don't know that I've got much of a head for heights, either. But I wouldn't mind snooping around up there.'

'And try to get to the other side?'

He looked at her for a moment. 'If you'd hold my hand while I climbed the shaft,' he said, easily. 'And on to the path itself. As far as you got today.'

'When do you want to go?'

'It'll have to be in daylight.' Then suddenly he said: 'What are we waiting for?'

'Now, you mean?'

'Why not?'

'I — I — ' She murmured incoherently, then pulled herself together. 'All right,' she said, 'I'll get my coat.'

He found Dan scribbling busily, his bed scattered with note-paper filled with writing. He looked up at Max and gave him a knowing grin which the other ignored. When he explained he was going out with the girl Dan sat up with a jerk.

'Going anywhere special?'

'Just the old copper-mine.'

214

'For Pete's sake you are.'

'Wynne's been explaining to me about this afternoon. About her uncle.'

Dan stubbed out a cigarette in the ash-tray, which was already half-full of stubs and lit a fresh cigarette. 'She knows we saw her?' And as Max nodded, asked: 'Didn't try to deny it was her?'

'On the contrary, she put her cards on the table.'

'Bit unusual for a woman.'

'You're just trying to be cynical.'

'How does her uncle come into it?'

Max said to Dan's reflection in the mirror: 'She's been worried about him for some time.' He proceeded to give the other an account of what Wynne had told him.

'What did you say,' Dan put in quickly, 'when she said she thought her uncle's death mightn't be an accident?'

'Kept my mouth shut.'

Dan relaxed visibly and Max went on to tell him about the plan of the old copper-mine and the rest of Wynne's story. Dan still seemed dubious. When Max had finished he said: 'So where she wouldn't risk breaking her neck, you're going to try and risk yours?'

'She has an idea she might find out more about her uncle.'

'You wouldn't like me to come with you — ?' Dan started to ask and then: 'No, you wouldn't.'

Max looked a trifle uncomfortable. 'I thought I'd go with her first,' he said. 'Then, if there was anything to it, you and I could have a look round later.'

Dan took a deep drag at his cigarette. He expelled a could of smoke slowly, frowning through it at Max. 'I only wish I felt sure about her.'

Max paused at the door. 'You think she may have some ulterior motive back of all this?'

Dan regarded him for a moment or two without answering. Then he indicated the evidence of the work he'd been doing on the bed. 'Remember your idea for the play?' he said. 'None of the characters being what they seem?'

'Except the heroine, *she* should stay true to type.' He threw the other a reassuring smile. 'I know I'm showing all the symptoms of having gone overboard for her in a big way. But I'm not blind to the possibility she may be kidding me along.'

Dan nodded, as if accepting the situation. 'It's only that we seem to have landed ourselves in a rum situation,' he said. 'Frankly I wouldn't trust anyone.'

'I'll watch out,' Max told him and went out of the room.

11

'Thanks for 'phoning, Sergeant,' P.C. Parry said and hung up. He stared at the telephone reflectively. So the post-mortem showed Jones' neck was broken *before* he fell downstairs. Heavy instrument had done the job.

Parry rubbed his chin. Looked as if those two *had* been on the right track then. His fingers tugged at his moustache. Yes, as he'd told Sergeant Morris, they should be back at the Crooked Inn by now. He'd be able to keep a discreet eye on the place, and no one would be able to get far without his knowing.

He whistled softly to himself. It was a case of murder they'd got on their hands. Murder . . . Well, P.C. Parry told himself, it makes a change and that was a fact. His ruminations were interrupted by a knocking on the front door. He glanced at the clock. Gone four-thirty. The knocking was repeated, whoever it was they weren't being exactly patient.

He yelled out that he was coming and went to open the door.

'Mr. Parry — Mr. Parry — '

The policeman regarded the young man who stood before him gasping breathlessly. He noticed his visitor's face was an unusually greyish pallor, for all that he was puffing from his exertions and agitation.

'Hello, young Tom, man. What's biting you? Dad's whiskers caught fire, or someone chucking bricks at your cat?'

But Tom Rees didn't grin back at him. 'Come quick, Mr. Parry. Quick as you can. There's a body — '

'A body?'

'The path to the Crooked Mountain. It's there.'

'Who is it?'

'Old Price,' Tom said. 'Hanging from a tree, he is.'

Price! Parry paused momentarily as he reached for his helmet. Committed suicide? From what young Rees said. Hanging from a tree. Now what the devil would an old blighter like Price want to hang himself for? He was so old it could only be a handful of years before he'd be making the trip to the little churchyard down the hill anyway. Had the news of the tragedy at the Crooked Inn sent him off his head? Yet why should that drive him to take his own life?

These considerations churned round Parry's brain as he hurried out of the house, slamming the door after him.

With Tom Rees muttering at his side, he set off in the direction of the spot where the other said he had found the old man's body. Tom explained how a sheep-dog puppy from the farm where he worked had got lost and he had set out to look for it. Normally he would not have gone so near the Crooked Mountain, he admitted. Tom shared to some degree the rest of the village's superstitious fear of the place. But he had glimpsed the dog heading heedlessly in that direction.

He had come across the body as he rounded the rock overhanging the path.

Forgetting all about the stray puppy he had turned and run for it, straight to

Parry the Police. The latter duly compli-
mented him on his good sense.

'You didn't touch it?'

'No.' The other shuddered.

'Then how did you know he was dead?'

Tom Rees threw the policeman a look.
'You have to touch pitch to know it's
sticky? I never thought about him being
anything else. And even,' he added, 'if I
hadn't been too scared to do anything but
run I couldn't have touched the — the
thing.' He gave another shudder.

Parry eyed the greenish tinge that still
lingered round the young fellow's gills
and gave an understanding nod. Violent
death wasn't a pretty thing to encounter,
he knew. He'd seen enough of it, in war
and in peace — that time, for instance,
when Vaughan the Baker's six-year-old
kid had got run over by a farm-lorry
down at Toll-Gate Corner.

They were hurrying along the path,
ahead of them the hump of rock, with the
topmost branches of a tree visible above
it. Parry glanced about him as with Tom
at his side he approached the bend in the
path. There seemed to be no one about.

Only the almost inevitable, motionless blobs of sheep on the darkening hills, and the cry of a bird darting overhead. When he and the other had first gained the path he had noticed abstractedly that its muddy, gravelly surface showed only blurred footprints. On either side of the path was grass.

Tom Rees hung back as they rounded the corner. Parry could not restrain an involuntary gasp of horror at the sight that met his gaze. Quickly and firmly he stepped close to the thing swaying gently from the softly creaking branch. There was the glint of a clasp-knife and he was sawing through the cord.

It needed no more than a cursory examination to corroborate Tom's first impression. Old Price was dead. Brusquely Parry commanded Tom to lend a hand. Together they stretched the figure out on the grass. They tore up some handfuls of ferns with which they covered the terribly distorted features.

'Wait here, Tom, and don't move. I'll get to the Crooked Inn fast as I can and 'phone from there.' The other gulped some incoherent reply. He didn't relish being left alone. 'If anyone should pass,' Parry continued, 'say there's been an accident and you're waiting for the doctor. Understand?'

Another unhappy gulp from Tom and the other headed for the Crooked Inn.

As Parry stepped into the lounge a few minutes later Roberts appeared from the direction of the kitchen. He stood there frowning at the uniformed figure in the doorway.

'You here again?'

'Unless I've got a twin,' Parry snapped.

'If it's Miss Anderson you're wanting, you just missed her. She's gone for a walk. With Mr. Mitchell.'

'What makes you think I wanted to speak to her?'

'Who else should it be?' the other shrugged. 'She's the boss here — now. I wonder you didn't see them as you came along.'

'Which way?'

Parry was hoping they wouldn't be going near the path to the Crooked Mountain. Wouldn't do for Miss Anderson to bump into poor old Price. Had enough nasty shocks to put up with without that.

'How should I know?' Roberts was sneering. 'I don't go about spying on where people go and what they do. Better ways to employ my time. Which is more than I can say for others I could name.'

Parry let the gibe go without comment. He had been wondering how to 'phone without the other eavesdropping.

In his haste to reach the nearest telephone to call not only the doctor, but more importantly Llanberis, he had reckoned without Roberts. Had Miss Anderson been there he could have told her he wished to 'phone privately and she would have kept Roberts out of the way.

Now he thought the latter had given him an opportunity of achieving his object.

'If I could use your 'phone,' he said mildly.

Roberts jerked his thumb at the office, the door of which stood open. Parry moved to the office, then paused as if a thought had struck him.

'Mr. Mitchell has gone out with Miss

Anderson?' In answer to the other's muttered affirmative: 'Where would his friend be?'

'Mr. Evans? Upstairs in his room.'

Parry smoothed his moustache thoughtfully. 'Perhaps you'd let him know I'm here? Say I'd like to see him, if he could spare a moment.'

Involuntarily Roberts' dark, unblinking gaze strayed to the office. Parry smiled to himself. He had neatly forestalled any attempt the other had in mind of listening-in on him on the extension in the passage.

Roberts gave a shrug. 'I'll go and tell him,' he said.

Half-way up the stairs Roberts turned to observe Parry at the door watching him. As he went on up scowling to himself, he heard the policeman move quickly into the office. He heard the door close and then the faint sound of the receiver being lifted as he hurried along the passage to the bedroom.

'Sorry to disturb you, sir,' Roberts said to Dan Evans from the door, 'but it's Parry the Police.' He jerked his head in the direction whence he had come. 'I told him you were in.'

Dan Evans put the typewriter he had been balancing on his knees on to the table beside him, pushing a sheaf of carbons, typing-paper and notes on to the floor as he did so. He grinned at Roberts.

'Brought his handcuffs with him?'

For a moment the other stared at him, then realised he was just attempting to be humorous. With only a faint glimmer of a smile Roberts said: 'I didn't notice them, sir.'

'In that case, I'll come down.'

Dan picked up the confusion of papers on the floor and with Roberts following behind him, went down the stairs. He saw Parry the Police just quitting the office. He noticed the policeman's expression was unsmiling as he glanced up at him.

'Get your call?' Roberts said.

Parry nodded. 'And I left the charge for it beside the 'phone.'

'Thanks, I'm sure,' Roberts said, his lips curling slightly. Dan paused at the foot of the stairs.

'You want to see me?'

'If I'm not bothering you, Mr.Evans.'

'No bother at all. I was only working. And if there's one thing I like when I'm working, it's to be interrupted in the middle of it.'

'I'm sure you must dislike being interrupted as much as the next man.'

'I assure you I hate work. Thinking out the plot's all right — you know, making the characters come to life in your mind's eye — I enjoy that. But when it comes to putting it down on paper, it's — it's blue murder.'

Dan caught Parry's gaze wavering and turned to see Roberts ostentatiously bent over a table which he was polishing, Dan thought, with extraordinary care so that he looked like an actor in slow-motion. Dan was between Parry and Roberts so that his wink at the policeman went unobserved by the other.

'Matter of fact,' Dan said casually, 'I was about to treat myself to a gasp of fresh air.'

Parry was privately of the opinion Dan's simulation didn't deceive Roberts for a second. All the same he fell in with the idea and said: 'Perhaps if I might walk with you a little way?'

'You might.'

'It's a nice evening. I hear Mr. Mitchell and Miss Anderson have gone for a walk.'

'Yes,' Dan answered conversationally, 'they have.'

They were out of the inn and proceeding at an ambling pace along the road. Parry led the way, and as soon as he was sure they were out of Roberts' earshot, he cut into Dan's inconsequential chatter.

'Very quick on the uptake of you, Mr. Evans, that was.'

The other grinned at him. 'I rather fancied you'd got something on your mind you wanted to get off your chest.'

'Couldn't have talked back there. Too risky.'

He was quickening his pace and Dan said: 'You're stepping it out very smartly.' He glanced about him. They had reached the beginning of a faintly trodden track across the rough fields. Ahead of him and to his left rose the Crooked Mountain. 'Where does this lead too?'

'Across this field,' turning off the road and leading the way through the space where the hedge was thinned out by use, 'there's a path to the old copper-mine.'

'The copper-mine?'

Parry glanced at him sharply, a tiny frown of suspicion drawing his eyebrows together. 'Why?'

'Er — nothing,' Dan hesitated. 'Just remembering the stories I've heard about it — '

'This is no story you're going to hear now,' Parry said. 'This is real.'

Dan saw the policeman's face was etched in harsh lines. His jaw was set and his lips grimly compressed.

'Now you're frightening me,' he said carelessly. What in hell he was wondering had this village flattie got on to this time?

At his mention of the copper-mine, Dan's thoughts had flown to Max and the girl. Had Parry been trailing them and discovered something?

Parry muttered to himself. Dan didn't catch what it was.

'What's the trouble?' he said, still trying to make his tone seem casual. If the other had found out something, Dan wasn't going to say anything till the copper had come out with it first.

'It's a body,' Parry said.

Dan stopped in his tracks, staring at Parry. 'A body.' He found his voice. 'Who?'

'Someone you know.' Then slowly: 'And it's got all the earmarks of murder, Mr. Evans . . . and that's a fact.'

12

There had been a very good reason why on his way back from viewing the body Parry had missed meeting Wynne Anderson and Max Mitchell. They had deliberately gone out of their way to avoid him. The girl had paused by the break in the hedge which gave on to the erratic track across the field.

'Think we should get to the mine and back before dark?' Max was asking her, as she glanced at her wristwatch.

'Quarter-past five. We'll do it easily.'

'Quite an evening coming on by the look of it.'

Max's gaze was raised to the Crooked Mountain and the grandeur of Snowdon's mountains beyond. The scene was changing colour even as Max and now the girl watched. The faint fingers of evening were touching the dark and lighter shades of green, drawing over the lower slopes and valleys the first hint of the mists that come with dusk.

'I could stare at them all the time,' the girl had murmured.

'Never understand why people want to *climb* them,' Max was saying.

'Seems a dangerous way of getting to know them.'

'I was thinking it's more their far-off grandeur that's so inspiring.'

'Distance lends enchantment to the view — '

Wynne had broken off at the same time as Max, his eyes suddenly shifting, gave a sudden exclamation.

'Talking of distance lending enchantment,' he had murmured, 'I don't think we need to get a closer view of Parry the Police.'

She had seen the familiar figure approaching across the field. He was walking hurriedly.

With a swift movement she turned back and with Max following her led the way down into a broad ditch alongside the road. They gained a hedge running at right angles to the field for some forty yards until, Max could see, it twisted to their right. If they kept their heads down they could avoid being spotted by Parry, while at the same time continuing towards their destination.

'He'd be bound to have nosed out where we were heading for,' Max muttered as he followed the girl, 'and tacked himself on to us.'

'Definitely a case of three's a crowd,' Wynne said over her shoulder. 'This takes a bit longer, but we can keep out of sight. By the time he reaches the road we'll have turned the corner.'

Her voice was a little breathless. Once again as he kept close behind her Max caught a hint of the elusive perfume she had been wearing last night in the starlight. Was it only last night? It seemed an aeon ago since he and Dan had arrived at the Crooked Inn.

'This is making me feel horribly guilty,' she was saying, a little laugh in her voice.

'Me too, I've always been secretly scared of cops ever since I was a kid.'

In a few minutes they were screened from the road by the angling of the hedge away to their right. They eased their pace and felt they were safe in walking without ducking their heads. Wynne explained the hedge ended about another thirty yards further on. They would strike a way to the path to the mountain.

Presently the hedge straggled to a finish. Ahead of them the ground began a slowly rising incline. The girl pointed out the rough path that twisted upwards and led the way across the rough field. They dodged boulders and holes in the ground.

They did not glance back.

They reached the path well beyond the rocky over-hanging shoulder that rose up behind them. Even if they had glanced back the tree that spread its branches over the path masked the solitary figure of Tom Rees standing guard beside the inert shape stretched in the grass. Tom had his back to them, his eyes intent on the direction Parry the Police had gone to the inn.

Max and the girl were soon climbing the lower slopes of the Crooked Mountain, scrambling their way up through the loose rock and shale. Max led the way now, taking her hand and helping her across the more treacherous patches.

Ahead where the rough path twisted upwards he could see the entrance to the old mine-shaft.

In a few minutes they stood at the cavernous opening. Max peered up into the darkness into which the shaft reached. It was a pitch-black tunnel driven at an angle of about seventy-five degrees upwards into the mountain, its sides supported in places by rough wooden uprights and planking. Similar supports bolstered the ceiling. At one time, Max reflected, staring as well as the darkness permitted into the shaft, the structure had been firm and sound. Now he could not help noticing much of the wood appeared rotten and unsafe.

'You took on a job,' he said to the girl, 'fighting your way up this.'

'It was a bit of an effort.'

Her eyes behind the slanting horn-rims seemed to hold an expression of amusement in them. Was there a faintly mocking expression in their smoky depths? He recalled Dan's warning. For a few moments her undeniable appeal fought with the murmurings of suspicion which lingered at the back of his mind. Would linger, he realised without admitting it, until the mystery of the Crooked Inn was solved.

He went into the shaft and began climbing, the girl close behind him. The floor of the shaft was stretches of rock broken by patches of mud and shale. The rock was slippery and the patches of loose rubble equally treacherous beneath their feet. As he scrambled upwards into the darkness, he decided the original users of the shaft must have possessed the sure-footedness of mountain-goats, and the tenacity of a mule.

He observed as much to the girl. 'How they could have done this climb every day — '

'Probably had ropes to haul themselves up by,' she thought. 'Or a rail of some kind they could hang on to.'

'Damned if I know how you managed it,' he said admiringly. 'Not knowing when your next step wouldn't bring the entire shaft caving in on top of you.'

'There are one or two places where it's

been braced up. Recently, too. Have you noticed?'

He halted his climb to peer about him in the semi-darkness. He'd been too engrossed keeping a foothold on the crumbling surface to have noticed anything else. But now as the girl pointed out some supports they had just reached, he could discern obvious signs of renovations. Fresh uprights and planking had been introduced to shore up what had been a particularly dangerous section of the shaft.

'You're right, too,' he said. 'I wonder who — ?'

His conjecture was interrupted by her sudden scream. At the same moment he caught the quick movement, a glint of an eye and a scurrying flash down the shaft.

'A rat — ' The girl was gasping with fright and he was close beside her, holding her steadily.

'It's all right. It's gone.'

'It — it was horrible.'

'You're quite safe,' he told her. 'In my arms.'

Behind her spectacles her gaze held his.

Her mouth was soft and tremulous, gleaming and close. A strand of her hair danced incongruously over her nose as she breathed quickly. Her body was warm and firm against his. She gave a little laugh and tautened.

'I — don't you think we should keep on keeping on? We must be nearly there.'

His hold slackened and she drew away and he began toiling upwards once more, reaching to help her close behind him. The shaft did not improve, except that it grew lighter and ahead of them they could now glimpse a hint of sky. In a few minutes Max was out of the shaft turning to give Wynne a final helping hand.

They stood on a wide, grassy slope of the mountain. From the shaft, the slope narrowed into a path for about thirty yards until it became no more than a ledge above a precipitous drop sheer into space.

'You can see where the path goes,' Wynne was saying. 'It turns round the rock there — '

'Which is as far as you got, when we saw you. Don't blame you. Looks like one hell of lot of empty nothing below.'

His gaze shifted towards Snowdon, from where earlier he and Dan had seen the girl at this self-same place on Crooked Mountain. In the gathering dusk Snowdon rose gentle and majestic among the peaks surrounding it. The mountains were darkening now with a faint purplish light. The rich greens and browns of the grassy slopes and the gorse seemed to have had their lively colour extracted. There was a faintly chilly appearance about the mountains, they were less inviting. An air of desolation seemed to lie over them.

Max heard a quick gasp beside him and turned to see the girl staring ahead of her. He followed the direction of her gaze and at once moved forward.

Ten yards away something was moving. There came a low groan. A figure which had been lying in a hollow scooped out of the mountain-side began to slide help-lessly on to the path. Max reached the figure, the girl following him.

They found themselves staring down at Miss Kimber.

The schoolteacher was bound wrist and ankle with rough cord and a rolled-up handkerchief had been pushed into her mouth and kept in place by her own scarf. As Max and Wynne began to untie her and remove the gag the woman's eyes flickered open. She stared up at them for a moment, her expression blank. Then her eyelids fluttered and closed again.

'She's alive,' Wynne exclaimed.

As if to confirm the girl's observation, Miss Kimber uttered a long shuddering moan and opened her eyes again. This time she stared at them, frowning, but the blankness was no longer there. She started to say something and made as if to scramble to her feet.

'It's all right,' Wynne told her gently. 'You're safe.'

'Take it easy for a bit,' Max said and even as he spoke she sank back on the path again with a moan.

'My head,' Miss Kimber pressed her hands to the back of her head. Then her eyes rolled up to meet their gaze once more. 'Ohhh, Miss Anderson,' she breathed painfully. 'Mr. Mitchell . . . thank heavens — '

She broke off with another groan, but it was obvious her senses were returning and she appeared not to have suffered any serious injury.

'Wish we had some brandy,' Max said.

'I — I'm all right.' Once more Miss Kimber's hands felt the back of her head tenderly. 'Only my head,' she said. 'It — it's splitting.'

She struggled into a sitting position. Max held her up, as Wynne took the schoolmistress's hands between hers and began to chafe them.

'Thank — thank you,' Miss Kimber smiled at her wanly. 'Such pins and needles where they were tied. And in my legs, too.'

'How long have you been stuck up here?' Max asked.

'What's the time? It seems terribly late.' Miss Kimber glanced round her and the darkening landscape. The effort cost her some pain and she gave another groan, moving her head gently from side to side as if to make sure nothing was broken, her skull not cracked. When Max told her it was getting on for six o'clock, she stared at him incredulously.

'Six?' she echoed, her voice weak and faint. 'Goodness . . . I got here about one o'clock.'

'And you've been out cold all this time?' Max said.

'Whoever hit me must pack a pretty strong punch.'

'Poor Miss Kimber,' Wynne murmured. 'You must feel awful. No food — '

'They obviously left me here to die. I'd climbed to the top of the shaft and stepped on to the path. As I came out of the darkness into the bright daylight I was half-blinded so I didn't see anyone. I felt a terrific blow on the back of my head and remembered nothing till I came round just now to find myself tied up and gagged.'

Max was eyeing her curiously. 'What on earth made you come up here?'

'I'd heard these stories about the mine,' she answered promptly. 'So I thought why not see for myself.'

Miss Kimber gave them another smile

which was childlike in its innocence.

Max threw Wynne a look. He wondered if she was also recalling the strenuous nature of that scramble up the lift-shaft. The sort of journey that had required all their effort and determination. Not a bit the job for a spinster schoolmistress to take on, and successfully. Max turned back to Miss Kimber with a mental picture of her as he and Dan had seen her from the Snowdon Railway, energetically tearing up the mountain. Obviously there was a great deal more in Miss Kimber than appeared at first sight.

'Seems to have been a darn risky thing to do,' Wynne was telling her.

'At the worst, I only expected to meet a ghost. Nothing so materially aggressive.'

Miss Kimber spoke with a little spirit. She was smoothing her dishevelled hair, wincing as her hands encountered the spot on her head where she had been struck. Wynne was thinking she wasn't altogether the popular idea of a spinterish schoolmistress. She said:

'We'd better get you back to the inn.'

'D'you feel you can walk a little?' Max

asked solicitously.

For answer the other pushed herself to her feet. She stood there swaying a little, and a moan forced itself between her set lips in spite of herself. Wynne gripped her by the arm and steadied her.

'Please don't worry over me. I'm much better. My head's clearing — and my pins and needles have almost gone.' She chafed her hands vigorously. Then she regarded Max. 'If it isn't being too inquisitive of me,' and he and Wynne thought they caught a twinkle at the back of her eyes, 'what are you two doing up here?'

It was a fair enough question. Max answered it without any hesitation. 'I had the same idea as you.'

'Oh, really?'

'All these strange yarns about the haunted mine intrigued me. I thought I'd like to find out what they added up to.'

Miss Kimber was staring at him, and for a moment he thought her expression was somewhat sceptical. Then:

'Naturally, being a thriller-writer,' Miss Kimber said, 'it's just the sort of thing that would attract you like the proverbial magnet.'

Max nodded. She'd swallowed his story it seemed, after all.

'And I insisted on coming up with him,' Wynne said.

'Neither of you have been here before?'

There was a moment's hesitation before Wynne said slowly: 'I have.'

Miss Kimber eyed her with surprise. 'You? Alone, you mean?'

Wynne nodded.

'She was up here before lunch this morning,' Max explained. 'Dan Evans and I happened to see her, when we were on the Snowdon Railway.'

The schoolmistress glanced at him quickly. 'You were up Snowdon this morning?'

'Very nice, wasn't it?'

'It was.'

'We saw you. At Half-way House.'

Miss Kimber's expression was completely disarming. 'Just fancy,' was all she said.

'We kept a look-out for you on our way down. But you'd gone.'

'I'd turned back. I wanted to see what the Crooked Mountain looked like at closer quarters.'

'So here we all are,' Wynne said.

'And how very thankful I am that you both had the same idea.'

'Thank God we did,' Max agreed.

'I'm sure I should have died.' She glanced at Wynne, then at Max. 'Where are you going now?'

'We were going to try and get round the corner where the path narrows,' Wynne said. 'We want to see what lies beyond the rock that juts out.'

'But I think we'd better postpone all that,' Max said. 'We'll turn back and see you safely to the pub.'

'Oh, but why?' Miss Kimber protested.

'We couldn't let you try and return by yourself,' Wynne started to say, but she was interrupted by the other.

'I could come with you.'

'I don't think you'd be able,' Max said.

'Look, I can stand on my own two feet.'

Miss Kimber demonstrated by standing with her legs planted firmly on the path. She made a far from fragile figure there in the dusk that was creeping up the mountainside and gathering around them. In her tweed suit and thick-soled shoes, she certainly appeared capable enough of accompanying them. Her face was admittedly a little pale, but her eyes held a determined light.

'I don't know — ' Max began doubtfully.

'If I can't come with you, I shall follow by myself.'

'Really, you oughtn't, Miss Kimber,' Wynne said, but with less firmness in her voice.

'I've got this far, I'm not going to be deterred by a knock on the head.'

'Tough, eh?' Wynne said with a laugh.

'Oh, we schoolteachers are,' Miss Kimber said a trifle absently, as if her thoughts had strayed. Then she caught Max's glance bent on her. 'We are tough,' she reiterated. 'I promise I won't be a nuisance.'

Max said nothing, it was Wynne who said: 'I'm sure you won't.'

'All right?' Miss Kimber was asking Max.

He shrugged. 'If you really feel up to it.'

'So very kind of you both,' Miss Kimber said primly.

As they set off along the path, Max was turning over in his mind the implications of this attack on Miss Kimber. Who the devil would want to knock her out, he asked himself, then leave her bound and gagged? Unless she could have got free — and the tying-up and gagging had obviously been the job of an expert — she would, but for his and the girl's fortuitous arrival on the scene, almost certainly have died of exposure and exhaustion. The chances of her being discovered in time in that inaccessible place, with its sinister reputation, were remote.

They had reached the point a few yards from the overhanging shoulder of rock where the path narrowed rapidly, until it was only a yard wide. Max dragged his thoughts away from the puzzle that was perplexing him and concentrated on the immediate future. It did not inspire him with a sense of overwhelming exhilaration. Above, the mountain-side reached up in a steep wall. Sheer rock-face broken by narrow ledges where it had been smoothly sloping grass. The path on which they were now standing lipped over, as it passed round the shoulder, nothing more or less than a precipice.

Max thought it couldn't have looked more uninviting. The fact that although the light still remained clear enough, it was not bright daylight, didn't, to his mind, improve the situation. The idea of the girl, not to mention Miss Kimber, attempting those few but dangerous yards filled him with apprehension. He did not exactly relish the notion even for himself. He was not at all heartened to hear Wynne observe:

'Somehow it doesn't look so frightening now.'

'There you are, Mr. Mitchell,' Miss Kimber, who was directly behind him, Wynne following her, said: 'see what a difference your presence makes to we weak women.'

'The rock does bulge over a bit,' was all Max could reply as he surveyed the prospect facing them with a dubious eye. Over his shoulder he said to Miss

Kimber: 'What do you think of it?'

'Doesn't bother me,' she answered brightly. She indicated with a negligent wave of a hand the yawning drop beneath them. 'I've got a good head for heights.'

'I must say the rock looks as if it might topple over at any minute,' Wynne said slowly.

'I expect it's stood balanced like that for centuries,' was Miss Kimber's cheerful response.

'I'm sure it has,' Max said, managing to infuse some conviction into his voice. 'Probably stay that way for a few more centuries too.'

It was apparent Miss Kimber was not in the least daunted by the path's narrowness, or by the insecure appearance of the bulging rock shoulder above them. At the slightest show of hesitation on his part, the schoolmistress would, Max knew, eagerly offer to lead the way. It was up to him not to hint for a moment that the situation presented the smallest danger. That might undermine their confidence, with added risk to themselves.

'I'll lead on, shall I?' he said casually. 'Keep as close to the side as you can.'

He thought he could feel the path beneath his feet sag a little as he stepped forward, but deciding it was merely his imagination getting the better of him, he went on. Miss Kimber kept close behind him and Wynne, with a little gasp, following, pressing against the rocky wall rising above them.

13

Dan Evans stood silently staring at the pathetically crumpled figure in the grass beside the path. From the corner of his eye he could see swinging gently from the creaking branch above, the rope's-end from which the old man had been cut down. He turned to Parry the Police standing at his elbow.

Parry heaved a heavy sigh. 'To think I'll never be able to nab him for poaching, after all. And him such a sly one for the rabbits.'

On their way to the scene, he had explained to Dan how Tom had made his shocking discovery. On arrival at the spot he had sent young Rees off, warning him not to breathe a word to a soul about the tragedy. Vowing he would keep his mouth tight as an oyster Tom had hurried off back to the farm, only too thankful to get away.

Now Parry was awaiting the arrival of

the doctor and the Llanberis police, both of whom he had 'phoned from the Crooked Inn. Dr. Griffiths should be here at any moment, Parry had made it sound urgent enough, without telling him what had happened. You couldn't trust these telephone-girls not to be listening with all their ears, and then the news would be all over the place in no time.

'But surely it's much more possible that Price committed suicide?' Dan was frowning. 'What makes you think it's — ?'

'It isn't suicide and it isn't an accident.'

'Who the devil would want to — to — murder a harmless old codger like Price?'

'Perhaps it was the same person who did in Josh Jones.'

Dan shot the other a look. 'So now you think he *was* murdered?'

Parry pursed his lips as if he had said too much. He jerked his head towards the still shape in the grass, its face still masked by fern-leaves. 'This makes it seem more likely.'

Dan shook his head. 'I don't know . . . The whole business is getting beyond me.'

The policeman eyed him thoughtfully from beneath the shadows of his helmet. He gave his moustache a tug and shifted uneasily from one foot to another. 'It's getting a bit too much for me, I don't mind telling you.' His voice took on an almost peevish tone as he went on. 'Little village like Mynydd Llanberis having two murders in one day.'

Dan nodded. Then as if still not prepared to face up to the facts he said: 'You don't think he could have done it himself? I mean he might have had some reason we don't know about — '

Parry answered him in the tone of a forbearing parent addressing an ignorant child.

'Should I have dragged you out here, just for you to look at some old crack-brain who'd taken his own life?'

Dan considered this for a moment then turned to the other with a grimace of agreement. A thought struck him. 'Incidentally, why *did* you bring me along to this grisly scene?'

Parry's face might have been carved of wood, his moustache made of brush-hairs drooping over his mouth that had become a thin line. His hand seemed to become alive of its own volition, as if it did not belong to his body, as he reached with a jerky movement into his pocket. Then he was holding a scrap of white under Dan's nose.

'What have you got there?'

'It's a piece of handkerchief.'

'Handkerchief?' Dan looked up to meet the other's stony gaze.

'I found it clenched in old Price's fist.'

Dan's expression sharpened. 'You mean — ?'

'As if he'd grasped it while struggling with whoever it was killed him.'

It was obvious Parry was not without some inkling of identity of the flimsy scrap's owner. He was merely waiting for Dan to put the question to him. Dan duly obliged.

'You know whose it is?'

'As it happens there are some initials in the corner.'

'If it's mine,' Dan told him with an attempt at humour, 'someone must have pinched it.'

'It doesn't look as if it was a man's handkerchief,' Parry said gravely.

'Let's me out. Whose then?'

Parry was staring past him, however, and Dan turned to follow the direction of his gaze. Came the sound of a car drawing to a stop in the road.

'Be Dr. Griffiths,' Parry said. 'Know the noise of his old bone-shaker anywhere.'

Dan turned back to him with a nod at the glimpse of white in the rough, reddened fist. 'Whose is it?'

'Llanberis shouldn't be long, either.' Then as if he had only just heard Dan's question he opened his fist and turned the piece of handkerchief over with a thick forefinger. 'The initials in the corner are 'W.A.' Convey anything to you . . . Mr. Evans?'

Those eyes were fixed full on him now, steely, boring into him, Dan felt, as he tried to think of the significance of the initials. 'W.A.?' he asked. 'W.A. — ' He broke off with a gasp. 'For Pete's sake — '

'I thought they'd ring a bell.'

'Wynne Anderson.' Dan's voice was a bare whisper.

'Looks like it might be a handkerchief she'd use, don't you agree?'

Dan stared more closely at the white wisp in that huge palm, with the initials worked in the corner.

'It's a woman's. But you're not suggesting she's had anything to do with — with — ?'

'Not for me to suggest this person or that.'

'You've suggested it's murder,' Dan said grimly. In answer to the other's non-committal shrug he went on. 'And your theory is this handkerchief's proof of it.'

'I didn't say so. I only thought it might interest you.' Before Dan could say any more Parry had turned to call past him. 'Hello there, Dr. Griffiths.'

Dr. Griffiths came hurrying up, his bag swinging in his hand, his face a little moist in the evening light. He was a trifle breathless as he threw a quick smile of recognition at Dan.

'Came as quick as I could,' he told Parry the Police. Then with a cheery grin. 'Your friend here looks healthy enough — what's the trouble?'

Parry was about to answer him then saw the newcomer's glance drawn to the shape in the grass. Without a word, almost without any change of expression, Dr. Griffiths dropped to his knee and bent with brisk professional movements of his hands over the body. After a few moments he stood up and glanced at the rope swinging from the branch overhead.

'Hanged himself, eh?' he said to Parry, his eyes down again at the body. He bent and pulled the ferns over the distorted face again.

'Er — ' Parry hesitated for a second, 'that's what it looks like.'

'Funny thing to do. Shouldn't have thought it of old Price, of all people. Not the morbid type, somehow.'

Dan was trying to grapple with all the crushing implications of that crumpled wisp which Parry had pushed into his pocket on the doctor's arrival. Suddenly the line of his jaw became purposeful. With a glance at Dr. Griffiths, who was still muttering to himself over the idea of old Price having taken his own life, he stepped closer to the policeman.

Parry glanced at him. 'What is it?' observing Dan's suddenly conspiratorial expression.

'What — ' Dan lowered his voice, 'what are you going to do about her?'

The other's eyes widened a little. Then he protruded his lower lip under the fringe of his moustache. 'Don't know,' he said non-commitally. 'Not until Llanberis tells me.'

'You'll stay here until they arrive?'

'Got to.'

Involuntarily Dan threw a glance along the path in the direction of the Crooked Mountain. He found Parry's gaze fixed on him again. He stepped forward and spoke into the policeman's ear, his whisper hoarse with urgency.

'And you realise what I've got to do, don't you?'

Parry's interest was taken for a moment by Dr. Griffiths making some remark which he didn't catch. The doctor seeing Dan was trying to engage the policeman's attention, remained politely silent. Parry gave his ear to Dan.

'What you've got to do?'

Dan nodded. 'Find my pal and pronto.'

'Mr. Mitchell. Who's gone for a walk with Miss Anderson?'

Dan didn't say anything. Just a quick nod. Parry the Police assumed an expression of faint distrust, an eyebrow beneath the helmet was raised suspiciously.

'Know where they've gone?'

'No.' From the corner of his eye Dan could see the doctor aware of the sudden tension in the air, regarding them with increasing curiosity. Then he heard Parry's voice.

'Then how will you know where to look?'

'I — that is — ' Dan fumbled his words. 'I might find him — '

'You don't sound very sure about it.'

'I'll find him.'

'And when you do?'

'Why then I'll — '

'What'll you tell him?'

'Warn him, of course.' Dan's voice was lowered again, with a glance for the other's benefit at Dr. Griffiths.

'About what?' Parry's voice was low.
'Her.'

Parry stared at him, his face coldly impassive. 'I think,' he said carefully, 'you'd better stay here — '

'But if she's — '

'With me,' the other told him and made as if to turn to the doctor. Dan grabbed his arm.

'But if she's what you suspect,' his words came out in a rush, 'my friend may be in danger.'

'And he may not. Chances are you'd make matters worse, and that's a fact — '

'But I *must* warn him.'

'And let her know the game's up?'

Parry started to turn away again, but the jerk at his arm brought him back to Dan.

'You must see that — '

'All I want to see is you stay right where you are.'

'But I tell you I've got to find Mr. Mitchell.'

Parry the Police's attitude became decidedly stubborn. His voice while it remained agreeable enough, had behind it a ring of authority. His back stiffened as he said firmly: 'Now then, Mr. Evans, we don't want any trouble.'

'I absolutely agree,' Dan rapped back at him. 'Which is just why I'm going to find Mr. Mitchell before it's too late.'

'Llanberis will be here any minute,' the other told him, in a calming tone. 'Then someone can go along with you.'

'I can't wait for anyone,' Dan's voice rose desperately. 'I'm going *now*.'

He started to move forward, but P-c. Parry stood immovable in his path. 'And if I order you to stay?'

'Order?' Dan's hands at his sides clenched into large, bony fists. 'Try and stop me.'

Dr. Griffiths had moved towards them, his face a trifle worried at the sound of their voices raised now acrimoniously.

'I will,' Parry was informing Dan.

'Don't be silly,' Dan made an effort to control his rising temper and impatience. 'You'll only get hurt.' The damned fool, he was thinking, why won't he see I've got to find Max before the girl . . . He moved forward, his hands held low, his jaw thrust out like the prow of a battleship.

'I tell you — ' voice rising in affronted dignity.

'Get out of my way,' Dan threw at him warningly.

'In the name of the law,' lurching towards Dan as if to close with him. Which was something he ought not to have done, for the next moment Dan, exasperation and a kind of anguish at his own temerity lending him extra strength, hit the oncoming jaw full and square. Parry teetered on his toes for a moment and then to the accompaniment of an exclamation of alarm from Dr. Griffiths, slid in a heap to the ground.

'You asked for it,' Dan glared at him breathlessly. As the doctor approached Dan shot forward, causing the other to throw up his arms to ward off what looked like an attack upon him. 'Another patient for you,' Dan yelled at him as he swept past.

Dr. Griffiths gaped after the rapidly disappearing figure. Then, shaking his head to himself, the doctor sighed and bent down to give Parry the Police his full attention.

14

'The path's widening again.' Max caught the tremulous gasp in Wynne's voice. Close behind him Miss Kimber was saying:

'Oh, yes, we've got past the narrowest part.'

She spoke without so much as a tremor. He hoped fervently she was right. The projecting bulge of the shoulder of rock leaned over them. Once round it the path should open out on to the slope of the mountain.

Miss Kimber cooed into the back of his neck: 'I think it's rather thrilling, venturing into the unknown.'

A sudden clatter of falling shale and small rock caused them to stop with a jerk. Max flattened himself against the rock-face and glanced back at Wynne who was close behind Miss Kimber. He thought her face had suddenly turned white in the fading light. But she caught his look and forced a smile.

'What would that be?' Miss Kimber asked casually.

'That,' slanting a look back at the way they had come, 'was just some of the cliff underneath us breaking away.'

'Are we all right, Max?' The girl spoke quietly.

There came another clatter of falling shale, not so heavy this time, but Max felt himself tense. He saw Miss Kimber eyeing him quizzically and he gave her a wink. She appeared as unperturbed as ever.

'Perhaps,' she said, 'our combined weight was a bit too much for that last bit.'

'Feels like firmer ground now.' Max said it with a certain amount of conviction. It seemed to him they had reached a firmer part of the path. It was as if they were standing on solid rock.

'I'm sure we've got past the worst of it,' Miss Kimber agreed.

'Good,' Wynne said. There was a decided lightness in her voice.

Max rounded the bend of rock, the

others crowding close behind him. The path widened out. He pulled up with an involuntary exclamation of surprise. He found himself staring at a level space that looked as if it had been cut out of the mountain. It was as large as a football-field. He could not remember observing the space from Snowdon, and he glanced up at the sombre-looking mountain which towered above them on the other side of the narrow pass.

It was only then he realised the mountain railway from which he and Dan had watched the Crooked Mountain was hidden from view. Presumably this part of the mountain was in turn hidden from the railway. Or perhaps some trick of light or contour of the mountain-side masked the open space from sight.

'Rather disappointing,' Miss Kimber said. 'Don't you think, Mr. Mitchell?'

He smiled at her. 'What did you expect to find?'

'Not just this wide open space, anyway,' Miss Kimber said. She was gazing round her expectantly.

'There is more than that.' The girl was

pointing across at a tiny hut which Max had already noted. It was pressed close against the side of the mountain rising steeply from the edge of the cut-out space.

'Anyone in it, I wonder?' Miss Kimber said.

'Might be a shepherd,' Max said.

'How could anyone get up here?' Wynne was glancing about her.

Max had to agree there seemed no way a shepherd or anyone else for that matter could have reached the hut, except by the path they had negotiated. The sides of the mountain all round appeared too steep. Though there might be some hidden crevice on the far side, Max decided, used as a means of gaining the hut.

They were moving towards it. Miss Kimber was murmuring half to herself the hut was bound to be empty. Max found Wynne was very close beside him. He felt her hand on his arm, and he could feel the pressure of her fingers. He glanced down at her curiously. There was a tautness about the corners of her mouth. Her eyes behind the horn-rim spectacles were fixed on the hut.

Without looking up at him she became aware of his gaze fixed on her. She said in a quiet voice:

'Max . . . '

'No one's popped out to welcome us,' he had started to say but he broke off. 'What?'

'Do you think we ought to — ?'

Her question trailed off. Her voice was low. Her fingers dug more deeply into his arm. He glanced at Miss Kimber on his other side. She appeared not to have noticed Wynne's sudden reaction as they drew nearer the hut.

'Ought to what?'

'Yes, ought to what, my dear?'

It was Miss Kimber who echoed him. She had been listening to Wynne after all.

The girl stopped suddenly and they both regarded her. Max frowned a little at her, but from the tail of his eye he could see that Miss Kimber appeared quite untroubled by Wynne's strange attitude.

'I feel scared suddenly. There's something about it — '

'Imagining things aren't you?' Max

said, his tone light.

'I — I think we should turn back.'

Wynne's voice was a little high, it held a panicky note. Her face looked suddenly white, Max thought, then decided it was merely the curious light of early evening gave her face that pallor.

'We must see inside it first,' Miss Kimber said. She gave the girl a sympathetic smile, then turned to Max for confirmation.

'Might as well, now we're here.'

'After all,' the schoolmistress glanced round, 'there's nothing else to see.'

Max put his hand on Wynne's fingers which still dug into his arm. After a moment he felt her relax her grip and he smiled down at her encouragingly. For the first time it seemed Miss Kimber saw her pallor.

'Has all this been too much for you?'

The girl forced a faint smile to the corners of her mouth. 'I'm just being stupid, that's all.'

'Hold on tight to Mr. Mitchell. You'll feel safe enough.'

Now they were only a few yards away

from the hut. It appeared rather larger now as they drew nearer it. It was built of wooden planks and stood about nine feet high at the front, with a corrugated iron roof that ran back, dropping about a couple of feet. A door with a window on either side of it faced them.

The windows had been broken and where the glass had once been was filled up with old bits of sacking. Max caught the faint creak-creak of the door and saw one of the hinges was broken so it could not be shut properly.

'Looks a very harmless sort of place to me.' There was disappointment evident in Miss Kimber's tones. Max gave a smile. Beneath her prim and spinsterish exterior the schoolteacher obviously possessed a yearning for excitement. He would have thought she'd had her share of it for the time being. But, no, it seemed, her appetite for thrills had only been whetted by the bang she had received on the head.

'We'll just take a quick look at it, and get back,' he said to Wynne comfortingly.

'It's a very broken-down looking place,'

she said, apprehension still there in her voice.

'Shouldn't think anyone's been near it for ages,' Miss Kimber said.

Max pushed the door wide. It creaked a lot. He went in, followed by the girl and Miss Kimber, who continued to chat away, behind them. It was gloomy, the only light coming in through a dirty pane of glass high up in the wall opposite the door.

'Not exactly a desirable residence with all mod. con.,' Wynne said. She was close to Max, who took her arm firmly. She gave a jerk of her head and he glanced at her sharply. Her profile was pale in the gloom, her whole figure tensed.

'What is it?'

'Thought I heard something moving outside.'

'I didn't hear anyone,' Miss Kimber said. 'Perhaps it was a bird, or a rabbit.'

They paused there in the middle of the dim hut. It was then Max noticed a rough table in the corner. There was a plate on it and a cup, its handle broken. A scrap of bread-crust lay beside the plate. He

271

crossed quickly to the table.

'Someone has been here.' It was Miss Kimber beside him and without raising her gaze from the table she picked up the remains of the crust. 'Recently,' she said. 'This isn't so very stale.'

'Perhaps it was the man who knocked you out.' Wynne had joined them.

Miss Kimber turned to her, blinking with a little surprise. 'Gracious me, I'd forgotten all about that.'

'Whoever it is,' Max said, 'they've kept themselves pretty scarce.'

He saw an oil-stove which had been pushed against the wall near the table. There was a kettle placed on the stove. It was black and battered-looking, but when he picked it up he could hear a little water slosh round inside it.

'We could make ourselves a cup of tea,' Miss Kimber said with a little laugh.

'Please can't we go?' Wynne said. 'There's nothing here — '

'Someone has,' Max said.

'Someone has what?' Miss Kimber said.

'Made themselves a cup of tea.' He

patted the side of the kettle as he returned it to its place on the oil-stove. 'It's warm.'

'Not long been used, you mean?'

'Max,' there was a fresh urgency in the girl's tone, 'let's get away. I'm sure there's someone — '

'It's all right,' Miss Kimber said. 'There are three of us — '

She broke off at Max's exclamation and sudden movement towards the other side of the hut. He stared at something black that glinted back at him from the darkness. 'A telephone. Who the devil would want — ?'

He reached out involuntarily to lift the receiver and see if it was working. A sound behind him swung him round on his heels, the girl and Miss Kimber too.

The doorway framed a figure black against the fading sky. As the three of them stared at it the shadowy face under the brim of the hat twisted into a snarl so that the teeth gleamed wolfishly. There was a flicker of steel-rimmed spectacles and then a movement of the man's right hand which held an automatic.

'Don't move any of you.' The thin-lipped mouth, the menacingly quiet voice.

Max said: 'Why, you're Vernon.'

'Recognise me, eh?'

The door creaked and swung back as he advanced towards them, leaving a thin streak of daylight edging into the hut. Miss Kimber put a hand to her forehead and swayed a little.

'I think I feel rather faint,' she said.

'Better think again.' The schoolteacher pulled herself upright as if the man had drawn the back of his hand viciously across her face. The oncoming steel-rims glinted then stopped. 'Any tricks like that and it'll be just too bad for you.'

Max saw that Wynne's face was like a sleep-walker's. Again that gleam of teeth as Vernon's mouth stretched in a smile. Max found himself thinking they must be dentures. 'And don't think I won't plug any one of you at the first funny move,' Vernon said.

'I don't see how that would get you anywhere,' Max said.

Now the mouth grew taut over the white teeth, the jaw muscles bunched.

'It'll get me as far as I want to go.'

'You realise, of course, our friends at the Crooked Inn know we're exploring the old copper-mine.' Max attempted an air of sang-froid he was far from feeling: 'They'll soon start searching for us.'

'I shouldn't be surprised if they have started out for us already.'

It was Wynne who spoke now, her voice shaky but her chin thrust forward in a show of defiance.

'They can find you, for all I care.'

'But I shouldn't have thought you could afford to let them find *you*,' Max said.

'I shan't be here.'

The dark, forbidding figure standing there, his suit creased and mud-stained, the flicker of his spectacles the only thing about him that seemed alive. He spoke in a flat voice, harsh with undertones of desperation.

'Where, just as a matter of interest,' Max said, 'will you be?'

'There's only one path, don't forget,' Miss Kimber said, 'the one we came by.'

'Which ought to lead you slap into our

friends,' Max said.

'You think you're all being very bright.'

'One needs to keep one's spirits up at a time like this,' Miss Kimber responded.

Vernon's malevolent gaze on Wynne turned to the other with a growl. 'Better not let yourself get too chirpy, or I'll quieten you with another crack on your bean.'

Miss Kimber's eyebrows rose. 'So it was you who attacked me?'

'Trouble with me is I'm too half-hearted. I should have pushed you over the edge.'

'Perhaps you'd like me to put in a good word for you with the police?'

Vernon eyed Miss Kimber in a moment of sullen silence, his automatic wavering in her direction. For one terrible moment Max thought he was going to fire. He could feel his heart racing and he ground his teeth together. But the man relaxed. All he said was:

'I'll keep out of their way, don't worry.' His gaze flickered from Miss Kimber back to Wynne, then from the girl to Max. 'As it happens there is another way of escape you wouldn't know about.'

'He's bluffing,' Max said. 'It's no good,' to Vernon, 'whatever happens to us, you will never make a getaway.'

Miss Kimber who had apparently been studying the wall above Vernon's left shoulder spoke quietly, almost absently. 'I'm afraid he will, you know.'

Vernon's spectacles jerked towards her.

'How?' Max asked her.

'That's it, you tell them,' Vernon said.

'I know the other way of escape for you,' Miss Kimber said slowly, quietly. 'And if no one gets here in time to stop you, you will make it.'

'You've taken quite a load off my mind.'

'But what other way is there?' Wynne asked. Max regarded her, his eyes suddenly narrowed. The girl still appeared slightly shaky. The apprehension still sounded in her voice.

The man's finger rested against the trigger. The slightest squeeze, the minimum of pressure, and it could easily be curtains for any one of them.

'By 'plane,' he said.

277

'A 'plane?' Wynne gave a little gasp. 'Swooping in over Snowdon — '

'There's enough room,' Miss Kimber said. 'Enough to land and take off again.'

'It could be done.' Max was seeing in his mind's eye the flat space outside.

'Which means,' Miss Kimber said, 'the 'plane would have to be here within the next half-hour or so, while there's still light.'

'Thinks of everything, doesn't she?' Vernon said. He threw a grin of mock admiration at the schoolteacher.

'Have to be a daring pilot who'll chance it,' Max said to him.

'Don't worry,' Vernon sounded full of confidence. 'He's got enough nerve. What he's paid for.'

'Then it's true?' Wynne's eyes were wide behind her horn-rims. Vernon's grin grew wolfish again, but he did not relax his watchful attitude, the automatic still held menacingly, low against his side.

'And it isn't the first time he's risked it?' Miss Kimber spoke in a quiet tone, and Max and Wynne were suddenly staring at her. 'Is it, Vernon?'

'How do you — ?' Vernon broke off, his face a mask of suspicion.

The schoolmistress was talking again. Her manner was incisive, her personality had suddenly gained in depth as she eyed Vernon levelly. She said to the girl:

'He's one of a number of wanted criminals who've escaped by this means. It's an organisation for smuggling wanted men to the Continent. A racket run by someone using the Crooked Inn as their H.Q.'

Vernon said through his teeth: 'Being quite interesting Miss — whoever you are — '

'You yourself were hiding at the inn last night — '

'Then Dan *did* see you — ' Max said.

Vernon only stared at Miss Kimber and said nothing.

'No doubt, you were brought here by Roberts.'

'Roberts?' Wynne's turn now to stare at her in utter amazement.

'To wait for the 'plane,' Miss Kimber gave Wynne a brief nod. 'Yes, Roberts is one of the set-up. Just as your uncle was.'

The girl uttered a low cry. For a moment Max thought she would collapse. As he moved towards her, Vernon's voice rapped at him warningly.

'Don't move, I say.'

'Better stay put, Mr. Mitchell,' Miss Kimber said.

'It — it's all right,' Wynne said to Max.

'I'm sorry if I upset you,' Miss Kimber said. 'I'll tell you this as well. I believe your uncle wanted to break away from it. He may have decided to go to the police.' She faced Vernon. 'That's why you murdered him.'

'How do you know all this?' Max asked.

'Yes, come on,' Vernon smiled unpleasantly. 'Tell.'

'I thought you'd cottoned on to it,' Miss Kimber said, wearing an air of faint surprise. 'I'm a detective.'

15

'Caught me unawares, he did,' Parry the Police was saying to Sergeant Morris. He shook his head to clear it and tenderly touched his jaw where Dan Evans' fist had connected.

Sergeant Morris had arrived on the scene, together with a police constable, only a few minutes after Dan had taken his hurried leave. He had found Parry sitting up on the path, with the doctor bending over him solicitously. While Parry still a bit dazed staggered to his feet, Dr. Griffiths gave the sergeant an account of what had happened.

Morris turned from the cursory inspection he had been giving the body of old Price. 'Bad luck,' he said commiseratingly. He eyed Parry, who was still smoothing his jaw. 'Feeling all right, now?'

Parry braced his shoulders and settled his helmet squarely on his head. 'Like to lay my hands on him,' he said.

Sergeant Morris nodded understandingly. 'Now I want you to take me along to the Crooked Inn.'

'Okay.'

'You needn't stick around any longer,' Morris said to Dr. Griffiths.

'Nothing more I can do.' And with a nod at them all the doctor returned to his car, waiting in the road.

Instructing his police constable to stay by the body until the ambulance arrived, which should be any minute now, Morris set off for the inn, accompanied by Parry.

'You don't expect to find the girl there?' Parry asked him. 'She won't have come back yet.'

'One or two 'phone-calls to make,' the other said cryptically. 'Then a word with the head-cook-and-bottle-washer.'

'Roberts?'

'He might know, for instance, where the girl and Mitchell went. And if the other chap knew, we ought to be able to pick up all three of them.'

'I'm wondering if Roberts couldn't tell us quite a lot,' Parry said slowly. 'And that's a fact.'

'Shouldn't wonder if you're right.'

Roberts must have heard them as they reached the inn, for he appeared at once.

'Haven't you got a home of your own?' he said sardonically to Parry. He took a cigarette-stub from behind his ear and lit it deliberately.

'Yes,' Parry said, 'but I like this place as well.'

'I'm sure we're very flattered,' Roberts said.

'I brought a friend with me.'

'I got eyes.'

'Sergeant Morris, from Llanberis.'

Roberts muttered something beneath his breath.

'You don't sound as though we're altogether welcome,' Morris said.

'Parry knows this is a house of sorrow,' was the unctuous reply. 'He's been here enough to find out all he wants about poor Mr. Jones' sad death.'

'I'm very sorry we're intruding on your grief.' Sergeant Morris spoke with simplicity. 'I assure you, you have my deepest sympathy.'

'You didn't call just to tell me that.'

Roberts' voice resumed its rasping note.

'We also hoped,' Morris said, 'you might care to give us your valuable help.' Roberts eyed him up and down, his expression openly hostile. 'For instance, perhaps you could tell us if Miss Anderson is in?'

'No one's in. Only me. And I'm busy, this pub doesn't run itself, you know.'

'When do you expect Miss Anderson back?'

'Might be a minute, might be an hour before she shows up.'

'You must have some idea where she's gone,' Parry said.

Roberts turned to him as if surprised to find him still there. 'I know no more than you. And if you don't know,' his tone bitingly acid, 'with all the snooping around you do ... ' He broke off. 'Miss Anderson,' he volunteered after a moment, 'went out with one of the guests for a walk.'

'When was this?' Morris asked.

'About an hour ago.' Roberts indicated Parry the Police. 'He knows all this. Called here, he did, just after they left.'

'I like to ask a few questions myself,' Morris said.

'Why? D'you think I'll tell you anything different from what I told him?'

'Why should you? If what you told Parry was the truth?'

'I've got no reason to lie, then or now.'

'I'm sure you haven't. In fact, you're being most co-operative.'

The dark eyes gleamed suspiciously at Sergeant Morris, as if Roberts were wondering if there was some hidden menace in the other's remark. But Morris's expression remained bland and guileless. Roberts asked him:

'Anything more you want to know?'

'I'd like to use your telephone, please.'

'He'll show you,' Roberts jerked a thumb at Parry the Police. 'He thinks this place is a public call-box, too.' He turned towards the kitchen then suddenly swung round. 'Here, wait a minute,' he said.

'What?' Parry said.

'All these questions you're asking about Miss Anderson. Nothing's happened to her?'

Parry pulled at his moustache and

glanced at Morris and Roberts' gaze shifted from one to the other. Morris covered a little cough with the back of his hand. Finally he spoke in a conspiratorial tone. 'You're an intelligent chap, Roberts. I think we can take you into our confidence.'

'Thanks very much I'm sure.'

Morris chose to ignore the other's sneer. 'It's the old man, Price, we're really concerned about. He's been found dead.'

Roberts' stare was unblinking. 'Price? But I was talking to him only a little while ago.'

'Oh, you were?' Parry said.

'How long ago?' Morris said.

'Before tea it was.' Roberts thought for a moment, his brow corrugated. 'About three-thirty.'

Sergeant Morris watched him take the cigarette-end out of his mouth, tap the drooping ash off it and examine the tip of it while he rubbed the ash into the carpet with his toe.

'Know where he went after he left you?'

Roberts raised his gaze from the contemplation of his cigarette-end. 'Well,

I — that is, I — '

'Better not try and hide anything,' Morris said, his features had hardened. 'This is a serious business.'

The other saw the two faces fixed on him. 'What are you getting at?' he said jerkily. 'You mean, old Price was — ? He was killed by someone — ?'

Sergeant Morris nodded. 'We suspect he may have been the victim of foul play.'

'Murdered?' Roberts' mouth opened, the cigarette-end stuck to his lower lip. 'Old Price murdered — ?'

'And,' Parry said, 'looks like you were the last person to see him alive.'

Roberts turned to him. His mouth closed, he shifted his cigarette-stub from one corner to the other. He hesitated, then as if making up his mind, he spoke to Sergeant Morris. 'He saw someone else after he saw me.'

'Who?'

'If you want to know, he said he was meeting Miss Anderson.'

Morris and Parry exchanged looks. Morris said to Roberts: 'Know where he was to meet her?'

'The footpath. The one that leads to the old copper-mine on the Crooked Mountain.'

Sergeant Morris eyed him narrowly. The dusk was creeping into the lounge, and smudging its corners with shadow. Somewhere a bird sang to the first star of the evening that gleamed palely in the grey-washed sky.

'Why couldn't he have come here?'

Roberts shrugged. 'Miss Anderson's idea, he said. It was something very confidential he'd got to tell her and she didn't want to risk anyone overhearing.'

'*She* didn't want anyone to overhear?' Morris looked a trifle puzzled. 'You mean she *knew* Price had some confidential news for her?'

Roberts' eyes were suddenly hooded. 'I'm only trying to remember what the old chap told me.'

'And you're remembering very well.' Morris smiled at the other encouragingly. 'Perhaps you can remember,' his tone was still pleasant, 'what it was that was so very confidential?'

'Well — I — ' Roberts blinked and stopped short.

288

'We're listening, Roberts,' Morris said.

The cigarette-stub, soggy and yellow, moved nervously in the mouth that had tightened. 'It was some idea he'd got about Mr. Jones,' Roberts said finally. 'That he — Price — had seen someone with Mr. Jones in his bedroom just before he was found dead.'

Sergeant Morris leaned forward as if he wanted his whole being to absorb every syllable that was being uttered. Parry had been waiting for the sergeant to say something. Roberts had stopped speaking. The silence was oppressive. Parry cleared his throat noisily.

'Suggesting he *didn't* fall on his way upstairs,' he said.

'I suppose so,' Roberts said.

'Why didn't you let me know this before?'

Roberts tired of the cigarette-stub and took it out of his mouth, squeezing it into an ash-tray. 'I never took the old chap seriously.'

Parry grunted.

'And so Miss Anderson went off to meet him?' Sergeant Morris finally said.

'I suppose so. She *said* she was just going out to get some fresh air.'

'She didn't know you knew she was seeing Price?'

Roberts shook his head slowly.

'She came back later, you say,' Morris said. 'Then she went out for another breath of fresh air with one of the guests here. That right?'

'With Mr. Mitchell,' Parry said.

'But you've no idea where they went?' Morris asked Roberts.

'I've already told you,' Roberts said, his voice was sharp. His face darkened irritably. But Sergeant Morris seemed to have obtained all the information he required.

'So our next step, it would appear,' Morris turned to Parry, 'is to find out where our fresh-air fiend and Mr. Mitchell have got to. I'll just make that 'phone-call.'

Roberts opened the door into the office. Morris went in and closed the door after him. Parry stood eyeing Roberts and after a few uncomfortable moments the latter muttered something about getting on with things and went off to the kitchen. Parry took up a strategic position commanding a view of the 'phone-extension in the passage. Behind him he could hear the muffled murmur of Sergeant Morris talking to Llanberis. There came the ting of the 'phone being hung up and the office door opened. He turned back as Morris came out.

'I made sure he didn't listen-in on the extension.' Parry nodded in the direction of the kitchen.

'All available men are out combing the neighbourhood for the girl and Mitchell,' the other said. 'And Evans.'

'I look forward to giving *him* a piece of my mind,' Parry said grimly.

'Not to mention increased efforts to pick up Vernon.'

'Seems it all ties up, doesn't it?' Parry said. 'Vernon, Jones, old Price, the girl . . . '

Parry followed the other's example and kept his voice low. They could hear sounds from the kitchen which indicated that Roberts' attention was occupied.

'If she is involved,' Sergeant Morris

said, 'what's the chap with her got to do with it? He impressed me as being the steady, sensible sort same as his friend. Unless, of course — '

'Unless, of course,' Parry said, 'he's fallen for her.'

Morris massaged his chin with a large hand. 'If he has . . . ' He let the rest of his sentence drift away on the air.

'If he has, you could say he mightn't be responsible for his actions,' Parry the Police said. 'And that's a fact.'

Morris gave him a sidelong glance. 'You trying to sound cynical?'

'Just my opinion.'

'Must admit it's difficult to believe a young woman could be capable of strangling Price like that, and leave him hanging to look as if it was suicide.'

'He was a pretty feeble old man, don't forget.'

'That's true. If we assume she did murder him, it follows she probably killed her uncle.'

Parry was recalling the girl. Her wonderfully coloured hair and those smoky eyes behind the oddly-shaped spectacles. Wasn't his idea of a girl, of course, he liked them big and broad-hipped and dark, like that girl on the farm in Normandy during the war. He brought his mind back to Miss Anderson. No, it didn't seem possible she could have murdered two men within the space of a few hours.

'She could have been helped by someone else.' Sergeant Morris looked at Parry.

'Who have you got in mind?' Parry said.

The other jerked his head in the direction of the kitchen.

Parry nodded. 'Seems to me he's been dropping hints suggesting she knows something about it.'

Sergeant Morris had crossed to the passage and listened. He could hear the sound of someone splashing about at the kitchen sink. Parry watched him. The shadows in the lounge were longer and more solid. He could not restrain an involuntary little shiver, as if cold fingers had brushed the nape of his neck. Roberts and the girl, he wondered, could they be in it together?

'And they may have quarrelled,' Morris said, coming back, still keeping his voice low.

'And when murderers fall out . . . '

'Or again,' Morris said, 'he might be deliberately trying to plant the whole business on her.'

'That torn piece of her handkerchief in Price's fist, for example?' Parry said, sagely.

'Rather coincidental it had to be the corner with her initials.'

'He having done the job all the time?'

'Not necessarily.' Sergeant Morris pulled at his lower lip. 'He could be shielding someone else. Vernon, for instance.'

Parry glimpsed the familiar figure of Mr. Darrell pass the windows and he gave Morris a warning cough. Mr. Darrell came in hurriedly, then paused with an inquiring glance at Sergeant Morris. Parry introduced them and the newcomer's face clouded over.

'Over here to do with Mr. Jones, eh? Dreadful business.' Mr. Darrell shook his head. 'Dreadful,' pushing the soft tweed hat he was wearing on to the back of his head. His plump face was pink and moist with perspiration. Parry noticed him touch a brilliantly-hued trout-fly that was stuck in the lapel of his leather-patched sports-jacket. He seemed to bring a smell of the river with him into the inn.

'How have the fish been biting today, Mr. Darrell?' Parry asked conversationally.

At once the other's expression became animated again. 'Not good, not good,' he said cheerfully. 'You a fisherman, Sergeant?'

'Not much really,' the other said. 'Prefer gardening — when I get the time.'

'Given up for the day?' Parry asked.

Darrell shook his head vigorously. 'Got a beautiful trout waiting for me under a rock back there. Tempted the devil with everything — '

'And he still won't rise?'

'Not he, Parry. But I remembered a fly I've got somewhere in my room. Never used it, called a Black Jim — don't ask me why — and I thought I'd try it.'

'You might do worse than use a good old-fashioned worm,' Sergeant Morris said.

Darrell looked at him, shocked. 'A *worm*, Sergeant!' He shook his head. 'I'm a fisherman.' He gave a rueful smile. 'Not a very good one, but at any rate I'm not a blasted poacher.'

Not in the least rebuffed, Sergeant Morris watched the other ascend the stairs. Then he turned and threw Parry a wink. It was at this moment that Roberts appeared.

'Thought I heard someone,' he looked up at Darrell.

'Hello, Roberts.'

'You're back early, sir.'

'I'm going out again. Back for dinner, usual time. I'm in a hurry.' He went on up the stairs, breathing a trifle quickly. 'Got a date with a trout, I hope . . . '

Roberts stood staring after the other. He muttered to himself: 'Him and his blessed fishing.' Then he pretended to notice the other two. 'Haven't you gone yet?' he said with heavy sarcasm.

'We're on our way,' Sergeant Morris said.

Roberts grunted. He glanced upwards again. 'Still, he keeps happy,' he said. 'And when you think he might go off any time.'

'What d'you mean?' Morris said.

'Sick man, he is, that's what. Slightest shock or any sudden exertion.'

'Yes,' Parry said. 'I believe he's not at all fit.'

'Heart,' Roberts said darkly. 'I came to see if Miss Kimber had arrived.'

'What about her?' Parry said. 'Miss Kimber,' he explained to Sergeant Morris, 'is another of the guests staying here.'

'All this violence going on. She's been out a long time.'

Roberts crossed to the door. He stood gazing out along the road. Morris and Parry watched him silently. Then he shrugged and came back. He looked round the lounge as if to see everything was in order. He studiously ignored the other two. Parry said:

'When you last see her?'

'Miss Kimber?' Roberts said without looking at them. 'This morning. Before she went out. Then later she rang up to say she wouldn't be back for lunch.'

'Any idea where she was going?' Morris said.

'Llanberis,' Roberts said shortly. 'Where you come from.'

'She hasn't been in for tea?'

It was Parry who asked the question. Roberts eyed him without expression. 'That's right. Isn't like her missing her meals, neither.'

Morris stood at the door. 'We'll look in again,' he said to Roberts. 'Or 'phone you. If Miss — er — Kimber hasn't turned up, we'll do something about it.'

Roberts' dark eyes were heavy-lidded. One side of his mouth curved in a sour smile. 'Going to have quite a lot on your plate, aren't you, Sergeant?' And he swung on his heel and went off to the kitchen.

16

Max and the girl continued to stare at Miss Kimber for several moments after her casual announcement. She could not resist smiling at their obvious surprise. They heard Vernon snarl:

'I get it. A blasted copper's nark.'

'Hard words break no bones,' she said. 'But for the record, you should know I'm a regular police officer from Scotland Yard, seconded to Liverpool's C.I.D. for this job.'

'I never did like cops.' Vernon moved forward a pace. 'And just because you happen to be a *woman* isn't going to stop me from blowing you to hell — '

'No.' Wynne screamed as the black automatic was raised to point at Miss Kimber.

'That's all a cop deserves.'

Max poised himself to make a desperate dive at the horrible, menacing figure. Out of the tail of his eye he saw Miss Kimber standing there calm and apparently unperturbed. Then he heard her say casually:

'You can relax, Vernon, that thing's not loaded.'

'What — ?'

'I've had a few lucky breaks on this job,' the other said. 'One was to get Roberts on my side — '

'You're bluffing.'

'He double-crossed you, reloaded that thing with duds.'

Vernon stared at her speechless for a moment, disbelief struggling with suspicion in his face. Miss Kimber moved towards him slightly, cool and casual. 'Stay where you are.' He shouted at her as if to convince himself she was lying. 'You're bluffing — '

She gave a shrug and still came forward. 'Like to pull the trigger?'

Involuntarily Vernon glanced down at the automatic. Had he been holding an empty gun all the time? He looked up again at her quickly. But Miss Kimber had made no attempt to grab the gun from him. She just stood there, smiling at him.

'The swine,' Vernon said through clenched teeth. 'I'll kill him for this. The double-crossing — '

There was a sudden movement, a gasp from Wynne and simultaneously a sharp cry of pain from Vernon. Even as Max, seeing a chance to help her, stepped forward, Miss Kimber had closed with Vernon for a brief moment. In the same movement the automatic appeared in her grip. Vernon was grasping his wrist his face contorted in agony.

'It's all right,' Miss Kimber said to Wynne, who was looking at her blankly. 'We have to learn a spot of ju-jitsu.' And she threw Max a wink.

'But you just said the gun — ' Max looked blank.

'He hit the mark when he said I was bluffing,' she said. Vernon, still painfully holding his wrist made a move towards her.

'And to prove it,' Miss Kimber said, 'we'll let some air in at the window.'

A sharp report filled the hut, followed by a shattering of the glass in the window high up in the wall. Vernon stepped back hurriedly, his teeth bared. Miss Kimber glanced at the window and at the automatic with a grim smile of satisfaction.

'Sorry to make you jump, my dear,' she said to Wynne. The girl could only gulp. Miss Kimber, her eyes fixed on the cowering Vernon, told Max: 'That stuff about Roberts was pure fiction. You must use it in that play you're writing,' she smiled. 'Or has it been done?'

'You're terrific, Miss Kimber,' Max said. 'If that is your name?'

She nodded. 'We've still got to get this swine to the inn,' she said. 'Even then my job isn't finished.'

'But you've got Vernon,' Wynne said.

'I'll fix you for this, if it's the last thing — ' Vernon started to bluster.

'Shut up,' Miss Kimber said, 'and keep your hands raised.' She continued talking to Wynne. 'There still remains the head of this outfit to rope in.'

'Who's that?' Max asked. He turned suddenly. From the corner of his eye he saw Wynne put a hand up to her brow and shake her head dazedly. 'What is it?' he said to her.

'You all right, my dear?' Miss Kimber said over her shoulder. She had seen Max move towards the girl, his face suddenly anxious.

'I — I'll be all right,' Wynne said shakily. 'I just felt a bit muzzy in the head.'

'We'll soon be back safe and sound at the inn.' Max wished he felt as confident as he tried to sound. His eye caught the telephone. 'What about the 'phone?' he said to Miss Kimber. 'It's bound to be through to the inn and I can get hold of Dan.'

'If it's through to the inn,' she said, 'Roberts'll answer it.'

'But I could spin him some yarn, so long as he got hold of Dan.'

'He'd know where you were 'phoning from. He'd realise at once something had gone wrong for him and his crowd.'

'I suppose it is a risk.'

'You've got nothing to worry about,' she said reassuringly. She jerked her gun at Vernon. 'Start moving, you. And remember this is in your back.'

Vernon led the way out of the hut, his

303

hands raised. He was a pace or two ahead of Miss Kimber. Behind her were Wynne and Max. They crossed the flat portion of the mountain-side in the gathering dusk and reached the path. No one spoke as they left the smooth grass and edged close to the face of the rock that swung out over them.

They hugged the rock-face. Miss Kimber appeared as cool and steady as ever. Max could only marvel at her control of the situation. In a few moments they would be approaching the trickiest part. The path where it had sagged ominously when he, Wynne and Miss Kimber had negotiated it before. Would it hold for the four of them to re-cross?

Miss Kimber was warning Vernon to step as lightly and cautiously as possible if he didn't want to plunge to his death. 'And as you're first,' she said, 'you'll be the first to go.'

Suddenly she slipped on a piece of loose shale. She managed to throw herself so that she clung to the side of the rock and with a cry Wynne caught her. But in her effort to save herself, Miss Kimber dropped the automatic.

For a breathless moment the three of them watched the gun skid along the path. It seemed it must disappear over the precipice, when Vernon, turning round, made a grab at the gun. He caught it just before it vanished into space and then staggered back against the cliff-face.

For one moment Max thought he must topple off the path. But Vernon's luck held. Now he leaned against the side of the cliff, breathing heavily, but the gun pointing at them. They could scarcely believe it had happened. The tables were turned on them with a vengeance.

'Now, then,' Vernon grated, 'it's my turn. And this time I'm going to settle all of you.'

'You won't get away with it,' Miss Kimber said.

'Who's to stop me?' In the gloom, the other's teeth gleamed white, his steel-rimmed spectacles flashed.

'You — you can't shoot us in cold blood,' Wynne said.

'She was going to.' Vernon jerked the gun at Miss Kimber.

'Only if you tried to escape.'

A curious expression flitted across Vernon's face. Then his wolfish grin widened. 'And if I promise I won't shoot,' he said, 'will you obey *me*?'

'What d'you mean?' Miss Kimber said.

'It'll be very simple.'

Max's blood ran cold as he stared at that face, its expression exultant and evil. 'What do you want us to do?' He heard his voice as if it was someone else asking the question.

'All you have to do,' Vernon said, edging towards them, 'is keep moving. All three of you.'

'You mean, back?' Max said.

'I mean back.' The other held the automatic close to his hip. 'Backwards — *over the edge*.'

'You're going to force us over the cliff.' Miss Kimber's words were a hoarse whisper.

'You catch on quick,' Vernon said.

'You monster — ' Max made as if to lunge at him, but the gun shifted to aim at his stomach.

'I'll pump you full of daylight,' Vernon

said. 'Start moving. Back. Go on, each of you.'

'We'll be smashed to pieces,' Wynne choked.

'That way or by a bullet — what's the difference?' Vernon said.

The three of them stood there for a moment facing that terrible figure bearing down on them. Behind them the black, shadowed abyss. Only a pace would send them hurtling down to almost certain death. Then suddenly Max caught a sound behind Vernon, further along the path. The faint rattle of falling stones.

'Listen,' he said. His gaze shifted to a spot beyond Vernon's shoulder. The man grinned at him mirthlessly.

'Thought you heard someone behind me? You're not fooling me with that one.'

'I thought — ' Max was staring as if mesmerised past Vernon.

'Save yourself the trouble,' Vernon said. 'Move, I tell you — '

'I won't,' Wynne said, through her teeth.

Vernon halted. In the dusk they could see his finger whiten round the trigger.

'You daren't do it,' Max said quietly. 'You know our friends are looking for us.'

'They'll hear the shots,' Miss Kimber said. 'They'll come running.'

'That won't be much help to you,' Vernon said.

'Shoot if you like,' Wynne said. 'I'm not going to throw myself over the edge — '

'Start moving.' Vernon's face was contorted. '*Start moving.*'

'Like hell we will,' Max said.

Vernon stared at them for a moment. 'So that's the way you want it,' he said. 'That's the way you can have it — '

There was a scrambling rush behind him, a great clatter of falling shale. Involuntarily he swung round. Wynne screamed and Miss Kimber gave a cry. A flash and a report that echoed and re-echoed against the mountain-side, then a crunching thud as a chunk of rock struck Vernon over the ear.

Dan Evans, clutching the piece of rock, bent over Vernon sprawled on the path.

'Dan,' Max shouted.

'That'll keep the basket quiet,' Dan said breathlessly, grinning down at

Vernon. 'Anyone hurt?' he asked the others. The girl and Miss Kimber were looking at him as if he were something out of a dream.

'Dan,' Max shouted again and gripped Dan's arm. 'Are you all right?'

'Bullet missed me by miles,' Dan said. Max was hanging on to him, speechless. He smiled at Wynne and Miss Kimber. 'Rescue in the nick of time. Just like a play.'

'Oh, Mr. Evans,' Wynne gasped, 'you saved our lives.'

'Anything to oblige,' Dan said.

'It was terrific,' Miss Kimber said.

'I was scared the noise of all that stuff falling would make him turn round.' He glanced again at the still inert figure at his feet and then weighed the piece of rock in his hand. 'Shall I give him another tap, for luck?'

'He seems quiet enough,' Miss Kimber said.

'Incidentally,' Dan said to her, 'what are you doing here? It'll be something to tell the kids in class, won't it?'

Miss Kimber smiled at him.

'Miss Kimber,' Wynne said slowly, 'isn't a schoolteacher after all.'

'No?'

'No,' Max said.

'Then what — ? No, don't tell me,' Dan said. 'Let me guess.'

'I'm afraid I've been deceiving you,' Miss Kimber said.

'You're not a woman at all?' Dan asked.

Miss Kimber laughed.

'I mean you're a detective dressed up — '

'Dan, you chump.'

Dan turned to Max puzzled. 'No?' He sounded disappointed. 'That was how it was working out in the play.'

'We'll have to change it,' Max said hurriedly.

Dan turned back to Miss Kimber. 'I get it,' he said. 'You're a woman detective?'

Miss Kimber nodded. 'All the way from Scotland Yard.'

'That's something we can use, anyway, Max,' Dan said. 'Eh?'

'Mr. Evans,' Wynne said, 'you're wonderful.'

'Just like him,' Max said. 'Never stops

thinking of the play.'

'Naturally,' Dan said. He turned to the girl, who was smiling at him. He thought she looked fascinating. In the fading light he thought her eyes were slumberously beguiling behind her horn-rims. 'How about you?' he said to her.

'What about me?' She raised an eyebrow at him.

'Who are you, *really*?'

'I see,' she said. 'What character have you got me down for?'

'The heroine, of course,' Max said quickly.

But she wasn't listening to him. Her attention was fixed on Dan. He didn't answer her for a moment. Then when he was about to say something Max butted in.

'Thing now is,' he said, 'to get back.'

'Yes,' Miss Kimber said briskly. 'That's the next job.'

'The path was what was crumbling when Dan was moving towards us,' Max said.

Dan turned from the girl. 'Yes, it didn't feel too safe under my feet. Isn't there any other way?'

'No,' Miss Kimber said.

'How was this blighter going to escape?' Dan wanted to know, indicating Vernon.

'By a 'plane,' Max said.

Dan glanced at him sharply. And Miss Kimber explained. 'There's one coming for him. Should be here fairly soon.'

'You mean there's a landing-field?'

'Just back there,' Max waved his hand. 'Space barely large enough.'

'Sounds a pretty idea,' Dan said.

'We'll tell you all about the set-up later — '

'I've got quite a yarn to spin you, too,' Dan said. 'Talk about our play, why, when you've heard — '

But Max interrupted him quickly. 'What we've got to worry about now is getting back to the inn.'

'But look here,' Dan said, 'can't the 'plane take *us*?'

'Who's going to fly it?'

'The chap who brings it, of course.'

'That could be an idea,' Wynne said with another admiring glance at Dan.

'Too many snags,' Miss Kimber said.

312

They looked at her. 'First place, the pilot's bound to be a tricky customer. How do we force him to help us?'

'We've got a gun,' Dan said.

'We can't threaten to shoot him if he's the only one who can pilot the 'plane,' Max said.

'Exactly,' Miss Kimber said. 'It's bound to be a small 'plane, we couldn't all go.'

'And even if we could bluff him,' Max said, 'once he was airborne he could land anywhere he pleased.'

'That's true,' Dan shook his head disappointedly. 'We'd be out of the frying-pan, etcetera.'

'We shall have to go back the way we came,' Miss Kimber said. 'Keep our fingers crossed and hope for — '

She broke off abruptly as a rising clatter of shale and falling stones reached them. It was from that part of the path about which they were apprehensive. The rattle grew louder, there came a loud slithering noise, then a dull rumble.

'My God — ' Dan exclaimed.

'Keep back,' Miss Kimber cried out.

Instinctively they all backed along the

path and flattened themselves against the rock-face. Dan grabbed the still unconscious Vernon by the collar and dragged him close to the side of the rock. The dull rumble became a roar, a few scattered stones and pieces of shale fell on to the path in front of them. The whole cliff-face shook and vibrated.

The great shoulder jutting out from over the path only a few yards away started to move. As the path beneath collapsed the huge piece of rock toppled forward, tearing itself away from the mountain-side, shuddering and groaning as if agonised.

A gap yawned in the cliff-face, the rock toppled further forward tearing itself out by its roots.

17

Sergeant Morris and Parry watched
Roberts disappear towards the kitchen.
The grandfather's clock struck half-past
six. Morris checked the time with his
wrist-watch. 'Bangor will be ringing
through. Maybe Caernarvon too, if they
have any news.'

'Will they 'phone here?'

'No, your place. I said there'd be
someone there, waiting, in case they had
any instructions.'

'Should we be getting along?'

'Nothing we can do here,' Sergeant
Morris said.

Parry jerked his thumb in the direction
of the kitchen. 'How about him? All right
to leave him on his little ownsome?'

'Don't know what harm he can do.'

'I was thinking,' Parry said slowly.

Sergeant Morris eyed him. 'Is that all it
is,' he said. 'I thought it was the
belly-ache.'

The other ignored the gibe. 'Wonder if Mr. Darrell's all right? I didn't hear him go out.'

'Why shouldn't he be?'

'Him being a sick man, I mean,' Parry said. 'He might have been taken ill upstairs.'

Sergeant Morris scowled with a touch of irritation. 'Got enough on our minds without worrying about people being ill. He may have slipped out the back way — '

'All the same, if you don't mind, I'll nip up and see.'

The sergeant grunted impatiently and Parry went quickly up the stairs. He recalled which was Mr. Darrell's room, he had once seen him from the road looking out of his bedroom window. He went quickly along the passage, shadowy now, the lamps not yet having been lit, and paused at what he calculated must be Mr. Darrell's door. He stood for a moment listening. There was no sound within. He tapped on the door. Still no sound. He knocked again, more loudly. No reply. He opened the door and stood on the threshold.

It was the right room all right. There were fishing-rods and tackle everywhere. But no sight of their owner. Parry stood there indecisively. Must have gone out by another way, Parry decided.

'Looking for someone?'

Parry started and spun round.

'Sorry if I made you jump,' Roberts leered at him. 'Guilty conscience, I shouldn't wonder.'

'I came up to see if Mr. Darrell was all right,' Parry said, angry with himself for allowing a defensive note to creep into his tone.

'I heard someone upstairs. If I'd known it was you, of course ... ' Roberts allowed the rest of the sentence to tail off enigmatically. 'Mr. Darrell went out.'

'You saw him?'

'Well,' Roberts said, 'I saw the back of him. He was in a hurry. That fish he was after, and I suppose hearing you still in the lounge, he slipped out by the back.'

'Oh ... ' Parry hadn't thought of the possibility of Mr. Darrell dodging out the back way. 'Sergeant Morris and I didn't see him, and knowing he's not too well, I thought he might have — you know, something might have happened to him — '

'He'll burst into tears of gratitude when he hears how you worried about him.'

'Fancy you're very clever, don't you?'

'Shall I see you downstairs?'

'All right,' Parry said peevishly, 'I'm going.' The other followed him along the passage, dark and angular in the shadows. 'Sooner or later,' Parry said over his shoulder, 'you'll find the police aren't such fools.'

'Oh, no? What about poor old Price? So busy accusing him of poaching you go and let him get murdered — '

'Oh, shut up.'

'Wouldn't listen to me,' Roberts said. 'But I know what I know. I been warning everyone there's evil to do with Crooked Mountain but all I get is mocking and jeering.'

Parry was about to make some reply when he heard Sergeant Morris downstairs calling him. He called back and with a last thrust: 'Sorry I can't stop to listen,' he hurried downstairs, aware of

Roberts' gaze following him.

'That Mr. Darrell you were talking to?' Morris asked him as he reappeared.

'No, it was Roberts. There are back stairs from the kitchen and out into the yard at the side. Roberts said he saw Mr. Darrell go out that way. He was in a hurry, he said.'

'That's all right, then.'

'I hope so.'

'What's biting you?'

Parry was pulling fretfully at his straggly moustache. He didn't quite know what was biting him. It was something about that room, he thought, and Roberts stealing up behind him the way he had. Had he really seen Mr. Darrell go out? It was possible, of course, that Mr. Darrell, anxious to get back to the trout he was determined to catch, and hearing his and the sergeant's voices and afraid perhaps of being detained chatting to them, had slipped out the other way.

'It's Roberts,' he said in answer to Sergeant Morris's question. 'Snooping about up there.'

'After all, the man's employed here.'

Parry gave a shrug. He might be barking up the wrong tree, perhaps he was allowing Roberts' accusation that he could have saved Price from being murdered to rankle. He followed the sergeant to the door.

'Looks like a lot of cloud building up over there,' Morris said, with a glance at the horizon. 'It'll be dark in twenty minutes. Make the search more difficult, and if it comes on to rain — '

'Who's this?' Parry said.

Morris gave an exclamation and with Parry close behind him set off to meet the trio who were approaching. 'The chap with them,' he said, his voice raised in disbelief, 'with his hands behind him?'

A tired voice reached them. 'Parry,' Max Mitchell called out, and now it was excited and triumphant. 'Sergeant Morris . . . '

Sergeant Morris and Parry joined Max and Miss Kimber, mud-stained and weary with their prisoner. No one noticed Roberts poised for a moment in the doorway of the inn. He had heard Morris and Parry leave and followed to watch them off the premises. At the sight of the captive Vernon, head sunk on his chest, defeated and dejected, Roberts' jaw had sagged with dismay. He ducked back out of sight and stood, indecisive and shaken.

What the hell was he to do?

He pulled himself together. They'd be here any minute. He would have to wait. That was it, he would wait and see what happened. He returned to the door and peered out cautiously. He could see them there, moving slowly towards the inn. The man with his hands tied behind him, Max Mitchell and Miss Kimber, Sergeant Morris and Parry the Police. They were still out of earshot. He decided it would be wiser if it appeared he had been in the kitchen all the time and he hurried off.

Sergeant Morris was snapping the handcuffs over Vernon's wrists. Vernon submitted sullenly, all the fight knocked out of him, a handkerchief roughly tied round his head covered the laceration caused by Dan's blow. One of the lenses of his spectacles was cracked.

Max said to Parry: 'I believe Mr. Evans owes you an apology.'

Parry smiling: 'I'm waiting for that.'

'Socking you the way he did was unpardonable. But I know he's truly sorry.'

'Well,' Parry rubbed his jaw reminiscently, 'if he puts it nicely — '

'I'm sure he will,' Max said. 'This crazy notion Miss Anderson was mixed up in it — Price's murder — and knowing she'd gone off with me — '

'Very natural impulse he should want to warn you,' Parry said agreeably. 'Next time I'll just remember to get my punch in first.'

Max smiled and they turned to Miss Kimber who was telling Sergeant Morris: 'Really, Sergeant, I didn't do it all on my own, you know. Why, if it hadn't been for Mr. Evans turning up — '

'Don't you believe her, Sergeant,' Max said. 'Honestly, I think your policewomen are wonderful.'

'A detective all the time,' Parry said, eyeing Miss Kimber admiringly, 'who'd have guessed it?'

'Miss Anderson and Mr. Evans are tagging along behind, you say?' Morris asked Miss Kimber, who nodded.

Max glanced back over his shoulder at the empty road. A slight frown appeared on his face. 'Miss Anderson was pretty well whacked,' he said. 'And there was no need for hurry . . . ' Seemed as if Vernon was not the only one who'd been bowled over by Dan's dramatic appearance at that crucial moment on Crooked Mountain. And Dan who'd suspected the girl of being a murderess!

'The day seems to be winding up quite nicely,' Sergeant Morris said.

'We were beginning to get a bit worried about you, too, Miss Kimber,' Parry said. 'But I can see now we were really wasting time.'

Morris turned to him. 'Take the prisoner with you. We'll return to the inn. You must be starved, Miss Kimber.'

'I wouldn't say no to a nice cup of tea.'

Parry took Vernon by the arm. 'I'll 'phone Bangor,' he said to Morris, 'to send over and collect him.'

'My man from Llanberis will be waiting for you, I expect.'

'Not much trouble left in him,' Miss

Kimber said as they watched Vernon being led away in the direction of the village.

'He had a pretty rough handling,' Max said, 'getting him down the old mine-shaft.'

'How about the 'plane, Sergeant Morris?' Miss Kimber said, as the three of them headed towards the inn.

'I'll 'phone Caernarvon from the inn. They'll take the necessary action to cope with it.'

'They might decide to let it land and take off again,' Max said. 'Have a 'plane follow it and see where it comes from.'

'Be for Caernarvon to decide.' Sergeant Morris turned to Miss Kimber to hear what had happened when the great rocky shoulder finally tore itself away from the mountain-side and crashed down to the rocks and shale far below.

'Couldn't believe our eyes,' she said, 'when we saw there was another sort of path, almost where the other had been. We clambered over it and were soon on safe ground. Wonderful luck.'

'Nature's a wonderful thing,' Sergeant

Morris said. 'Like, for instance, being able to walk in the moonlight, when there's no moon.'

Miss Kimber looked at him a little blankly for a moment. Then she smiled suddenly. 'Yes,' she said. 'I can't think how I came to make that slip-up.'

They laughed together, then Max looked back again at the way they had come. There was still no sign of Wynne and Dan. Sergeant Morris winked at Miss Kimber.

'Seem to be taking their time, the other two,' he said. 'You say they aren't far behind?'

'They'll be along any minute,' Miss Kimber said.

'Perhaps they've got plenty to talk about? After all,' and Sergeant Morris grinned at Max, 'all the best plots have a love interest.'

Max made no reply. He did not see Miss Kimber shake her head at Morris. The latter's eyes widened slightly and he looked somewhat puzzled. Then it dawned upon him he was talking out of turn and he started to question Miss

Kimber about her assignment with the Liverpool C.I.D.

They arrived at the inn and Roberts was shouted for. He was sent to prepare hot reviving tea for Miss Kimber, while Morris got on the 'phone. Max undertook the same role Parry had played, keeping watch to make sure Roberts didn't eavesdrop on the extension. Morris came out of the office to tell Miss Kimber that Caernarvon had been forewarned and were taking steps to watch out for the 'plane when it landed on the Crooked Mountain. In any case the 'plane would be followed to its destination. All that was being taken care of.

'They must have sounded pleased when you said you'd got Vernon,' Max said.

'They were quite pleased,' Sergeant Morris said.

'So all we want now is to nab the arch-villain of the piece.'

'Why do you look at me, Mr. Mitchell?' Miss Kimber said. She was smiling up at him from a chair into which she had slumped herself.

Max didn't realise he had been looking at her particularly. He gave a little laugh. 'I suppose something tells me,' he said, 'you're the one who's going to show us the last trick.'

Sergeant Morris threw a shrewd glance at Miss Kimber. 'I think you are a jump or two ahead of us, too.'

She spread her hands in a deprecating movement. Max observed again how strong and capable her hands looked. Much more like those of a police-woman than a schoolmistress. 'I'm no magician,' she said, 'but I'll do my best.'

'It's someone here, isn't it?' Max said. 'I'm betting on that.'

'Roberts?' Sergeant Morris asked.

'Isn't clever enough,' Miss Kimber said. 'Just the typical criminal stooge.'

Sergeant Morris nodded in agreement. 'Not that it makes him any less dangerous. If I got him in here now, he'd shut up like an oyster. Now, the one we're after is really smart.'

'And ruthless,' Miss Kimber said, 'enough to silence anyone who talked too much, like Josh Jones who wanted to go straight — and Price, who'd accidentally stumbled on some dangerous evidence. It was Vernon did the silencing for him.'

'Sounds gruesome enough,' Sergeant Morris said. 'But then,' to Max, 'you see, crooks in real life aren't so amusing.'

'Trouble is, Sergeant, if you put real life on the stage, audiences think you're overdoing it.'

But Sergeant Morris's attention was riveted to Miss Kimber. She had got out of her chair and was staring out of the window along the road.

'That the other two you can see coming?'

She didn't turn her head. 'No,' she said. 'Just looking at the road.'

There was something in the intensity of her attitude that struck Max. It was as if she was expecting to see someone walk in any minute, he thought. Who was it she expected? To walk in without realising the game was up, walk into a trap? She made a little movement and turned towards him with a smile.

'Here's your friend. And Miss Anderson with him. And Mr. Parry.'

'Left Vernon in charge of my man and come back to see what else is cooking,' Sergeant Morris said, then: 'Roberts is taking his time getting that tea.'

'So now we're all accounted for,' Max said.

Dan and Wynne appeared at the door, and behind them Parry the Police. Dan glanced across at Max, who was looking hard at Wynne. Parry started to say something to Sergeant Morris, but he was interrupted by Miss Kimber calling for Roberts. She peered along the passage towards the kitchen and called again. 'Roberts . . . '

No reply and Miss Kimber turned to Sergeant Morris, her face suddenly full of apprehension.

Morris saw her expression and dived towards the kitchen, Parry after him.

'He's gone,' Miss Kimber said to the others, a note of certainty in her voice. 'Cleared out — '

They could hear Morris and Parry charging back, their voices raised. They reappeared, echoing Miss Kimber's words.

'Why should he have hopped it like

that?' Dan asked puzzled.

Miss Kimber turned to him. 'To warn Darrell.'

'Darrell?'

'He's your arch-crook we've been talking about,' Miss Kimber said.

There was a thunderstruck silence. They all stared at Miss Kimber, who was gazing calmly at Max. Her eyes shifted to Dan.

'For Pete's sake,' he said.

'Mr. Darrell?' Sergeant Morris was scowling his incredulity.

'I was going to tell you — ' Parry started to say, but again he was interrupted.

'Roberts tipped him off,' Miss Kimber said simply.

'But he was ill,' Wynne said. 'We all thought — ' She broke off in bewilderment.

Miss Kimber shook her head.

'When I went up to his room,' Parry managed at last to get a word in, 'I spotted a torn scrap of handkerchief on the floor. Didn't think anything of it, till just now. That's what brought me back here. I thought it was Roberts who'd accidentally dropped it. But it must have been — '

'Darrell,' Sergeant Morris said. 'He could have stolen it from Miss Anderson for Vernon to plant on old Price.'

'Liverpool got on to him a few days ago,' Miss Kimber said. She took Wynne by the arm. The girl was looking aghast as the implication of Morris's words struck her. 'One of Vernon's pals in London gave the show away,' Miss Kimber said. 'But we couldn't be sure, that's why I started to look out for him. This inn was only meant to be the start of the trail. But last night's and today's happenings clinched it. And now he and Roberts slipping off like that — '

'They won't get away with it.' Sergeant Morris turned to Parry. 'Come on.'

'You can include me in on this,' Dan said, moving with Parry to the door. Max was close after him. Sergeant Morris threw a look at them and gave a quick nod of his head.

'You better stay here, Miss Kimber, with Miss Anderson. There may be 'phone-calls . . . '

'All right,' Miss Kimber called after him. 'We'll leave the rough stuff to you.'

'Only do take care of yourselves,' Wynne cried.

Max and Dan found themselves turning simultaneously. But the slanted spectacles seemed to hide the precise direction of her appealing gaze, they could not tell which of them was receiving its full benefit.

As Max gave her a reassuring wave Dan could not resist grinning at him frankly. 'What a climax we're building up to,' he said under his breath. 'Murder and mayhem brimming over and the two heroes fight for the girl's favours.'

'You go in and win,' Max said in mock heroic tones, slapping Dan's shoulder.

'No, no, you saw her first.'

'Yes, but you saved her life — besides, you carry the heaviest punch. Ask Vernon. And Parry.'

They were still laughing together as, following Sergeant Morris and Parry, they reached the beginning of the path to Crooked Mountain. A distant throbbing sound rapidly drawing nearer brought them all to a sudden halt, looking watchfully up at the darkening sky.

It was a 'plane flying in over Snowdon.

18

The two men gained the slope ascending to the copper-mine. They had been running hard and now their mouths agape for air and their faces running with sweat they scrambled upwards, slipping and slithering on the rough path.

Overhead the 'plane's throb-throb grew louder.

'Be landing any minute,' Roberts said.

The other gave a gasping grunt, turning into a curse as he stumbled. He would have fallen if Roberts hadn't caught his arm. They pushed on like men possessed.

'No sign of the blasted cops yet.' Roberts had thrown a quick glance over his shoulder at the path below.

'They won't be far away,' Darrell said. 'Trouble is they know we're certain to make for here.'

His words caused Roberts to accelerate his speed. He was first at the top of the slope and staggering as if about to collapse he reached the entrance to the mine-shaft. He turned as Darrell, blinking the sweat out of his eyes, joined him. Roberts was listening intently.

'Can't hear the 'plane any more. Must have landed.' He turned into the entrance to the mine. 'I'll lead the way.'

'Not so fast.' The other's hand clawed his shoulder. 'I'll go first.'

Darrell's stubby fingers dug hard into Roberts' flesh so that he winced with pain. 'I was only kidding I'm an invalid. Remember?'

Roberts started to protest, but Darrell said between his teeth: '*I'll go first.*'

Roberts resisted as Darrell tried to pull him aside. His dark eyes filled with suspicion. He thrust his jaw forward. 'What's the idea?'

'Only you're not hearing so good.'

With a jerk of his hand Darrell pulled the other out of his path. The movement weakened his grip and Roberts twisted his shoulder free. He pushed himself in front of Darrell aggressively. 'Just a minute.'

'We haven't got all night to chat.'

Roberts could glimpse part of the path

below. There was no one in sight. His eyes flickered back to Darrell. 'Time enough to settle one thing.'

'Talk to yourself if you want. I'm on my way.'

'Wait.'

Darrell's face contorted. He spluttered with rage. It was Roberts' turn to grip him. He wrenched himself free.

'I don't like a little thought that's come into my head,' Roberts said. 'The thought that the 'plane's only meant to take one passenger.'

'It'll come back for you.'

Roberts leered into the other's face. 'Now isn't that considerate of you.'

The other drew back with a sudden movement and unleashed his fist with terrific force into the other's face. There was a horrible crunch of breaking bone and with a scream of agony Roberts' hands flew to his nose. Blood was pouring from it. As he rocked backwards against the doorway of the shaft Darrell hit him again with a devastating punch in the stomach. Roberts doubled up, his hands still to his face, the blood dripping through his fingers. Darrell steadied himself and crashed his fist against the other's ear. Roberts keeled over and pitched headlong. Darrell delivered a cruel kick against his temple and Roberts lay silent.

Darrell began climbing.

Now he was nearing the top of the shaft, the grey gleam of the evening sky only a few yards ahead of him. He cursed to himself as he scrambled and fought his way upwards. Mud caked his face and clothes, his hands were begrimed, his finger-nails broken. Above his laboured breathing the rattle and clatter of falling shale and rock fragments echoed back at him.

Another sound from below came to him. He paused for a moment, his features a malevolent mask. A voice that was half a groan and half a shout reached up.

'I'll get you . . . You swine . . . I'll get you.'

Darrell started his feverish scramble again. Then the toe of his shoe seeking a foothold found a jutting piece of rock. As he tested it with his weight it gave ominously and he pulled his foot away fast. Then a thin smile flitted across his face. He looked down at where his foot had been. He found a firm foothold a little higher up, but which enabled him still to reach the loose edge of rock. Roberts' voice, hysterical and sobbing in pain and fury, sounded nearer.

'We'll see who gets away first . . . We'll see, you swine . . . '

Darrell pressed heavily downwards. The jutting piece of rock sagged. There was a heavy fall of mud and stones. Curses and cries rose from below. But Roberts continued his ascent. Darrell's mirthless grin widened across his mud-caked face. Unhurriedly he kicked again at the edge of rock. It shifted again. He gave the protruding piece another downward shove. He felt it give and grabbed wildly with his hands above at the shaft-side. For a moment he almost lost his grip and would have plunged backwards. He held on, teeth clenched.

There was a rushing noise beneath

him, then an increasing fall of stones, more curses and cries from Roberts. Then a dull, tearing sound as the slab of rock gave way beneath the weight of the mine-shaft above it, a part of the side where the wooden supports were rotted. There was a loud rending noise and the entire side of the shaft below him started to slide downwards in a roar. Darrell, holding on frantically, eyes staring up at the pale circle which was his goal, heard the rumble and clatter of plunging rocks, mud and rotten wood. A thin, falling scream came up to him and then silence. He scrambled on upwards to the circle of light.

The collapse of the lower part of the mine coincided with the arrival, only a few yards from the entrance, of Sergeant Morris and Parry, closely followed by Max and Dan. All four of them breathing heavily, they were brought to an abrupt halt as fragments of rock and mud crashed down and choked the entrance to the shaft.

'It's those two,' Parry said. 'Must have brought the whole thing down.'

339

vas just about ready for it,' Max

Sergeant Morris eyed the shaft-entrance grimly. There seemed to be no way of reaching the place where the plane, whose engine they had heard cut out several minutes before, had landed. The fall inside the shaft ceased.

It was Dan who saw the foot projecting out of the rubble. Swiftly the four of them worked to drag the crumpled figure from under the mass of mud, broken wood and rocks.

'He's had it,' Parry said.

'No one could have lived beneath that avalanche,' Dan said.

Sergeant Morris started to clamber over the rubble they had dislodged and ducked a yard or so into the entrance to the shaft, trying to crane his neck upwards. 'Darrell seems to have been the lucky one.'

'He may be somewhere under this lot, too,' Parry said.

The light was now getting so bad, Sergeant Morris considered the advisability of sending for storm-lanterns. It would

340

be dark very shortly. He ducked out of the shaft and with the others who had lifted Roberts' crushed, lifeless form beside the path, glanced skywards.

'The 'plane again,' Dan said.

The familiar throb-throb grew louder, thrown back at them by the mountains. Sergeant Morris pushed the back of his hand over his eyes in a gesture of defeat.

'Means Darrell's in it.'

'The pilot must have had guts to take off in this light,' Max said.

'Darrell would risk it,' Sergeant Morris said. 'The swine — beaten us.'

'We'll get him yet,' Parry said.

Sergeant Morris had turned and hurried down the incline in order to get a sight of the 'plane. The sound of its engine was receding. The others followed him, stumbling and sliding down the rough path.

'There it is,' Dan said.

They followed the direction of his gaze. In the darkness closing round the mountains they could just discern the 'plane suspended for a moment against a patch of sky like some insect. Then it

341

seemed to disappear into the purplish-black mass that was Snowdon itself. Its echo mocked them.

'Pipped on the post,' Dan said.

Sergeant Morris's face was bitter. He swore fluently under his breath.

'I'm not so sure.' It was Parry the Police who spoke quietly. The others turned to him sharply. 'Listen,' he said.

'Oh, we'll pick him up all right,' Sergeant Morris said. 'I know. It's just the idea of the devil slipping through our fingers.'

'I'm not so sure,' Parry said still in his quiet voice, 'it'll gain height.'

Tensed and silent they stared up in the direction of the 'plane, whose throb continued to come back at them from the distant darkness. Then suddenly there was a brilliant flash, followed by a terrific explosion. The flare of red and yellow illuminated the tip of Snowdon in brief searing flame then died down into a glowing pin-point. It seemed to be all over in a second.

'My God,' Sergeant Morris said.

Their eyes were fixed unblinkingly on

the faint distant glow, like a cigarette-end high up in the blackness of the mountain-tip, silhouetted against the blue-grey of oncoming night.

'He didn't make it after all.' Max was the first to speak. His voice was low.

'Roberts, and now him,' Parry said. 'The wages of sin is death . . . and that's a fact.'

'For Pete's sake,' Dan whispered. 'What a curtain.'

THE END

We do hope that you have enjoyed reading this large print book.

Did you know that all of our titles are available for purchase?

We publish a wide range of high quality large print books including:
Romances, Mysteries, Classics
General Fiction
Non Fiction and Westerns

Special interest titles available in large print are:
The Little Oxford Dictionary
Music Book, Song Book
Hymn Book, Service Book

Also available from us courtesy of Oxford University Press:
Young Readers' Dictionary
(large print edition)
Young Readers' Thesaurus
(large print edition)

For further information or a free brochure, please contact us at:
Ulverscroft Large Print Books Ltd.,
The Green, Bradgate Road, Anstey,
Leicester, LE7 7FU, England.
Tel: (00 44) **0116 236 4325**
Fax: (00 44) **0116 234 0205**

Other titles in the
Linford Mystery Library:

DEATH OF A COLLECTOR

John Hall

It's the 1920s. Freddie Darnborough, popular man about town, is invited to a weekend at Devorne Manor. But the host, Sir Jason, is robbed and murdered hours after Freddie's arrival. However, one of the guests is a Detective Chief Inspector. An odd coincidence? The policeman soon arrests a suspicious character lurking in the shrubbery. But Freddie alone believes the man to be innocent. And so, to save an innocent man from the gallows, Freddie himself must find the real murderer.

SHERLOCK HOLMES AND THE GIANT'S HAND

Matthew Book

Three of the great detective's most singular cases, mentioned tantalisingly briefly in the original narratives, are now presented here in full. The curious disappearance of Mr Stanislaus Addleton leads Holmes and Watson ultimately to the mysterious 'Giant's Hand'. What peculiar brand of madness drives Colonel Warburton to repeatedly attack an amiable village vicar? Then there is the murderous tragedy of the Abernetty family, the solving of which hinges on the depth to which the parsley had sunk into the butter on a hot day . . .